# FIRE IN THE BLOOD

# Fire in the Blood

## Irène Némirovsky

*Translated from the French*
*by Sandra Smith*

**ISIS**
**LARGE PRINT**
**Oxford**

First published in Great Britain 2007
by
Chatto & Windus, one of the publishers in
The Random House Group Ltd.


Published in Large Print 2008 by ISIS Publishing Ltd.,
7 Centremead, Osney Mead, Oxford OX2 0ES
by arrangement with
Chatto & Windus, one of the publishers in
The Random House Group Ltd.

**British Library Cataloguing in Publication Data**
Némirovsky, Irène, 1903–1942
    Fire in the blood. – Large print ed.
    1. Family secrets – Fiction
    2. Village communities – France – Fiction
    3. Memory in old age – Fiction
    4. Large type books
    I. Title
    843.9'12 [F]


ISBN 978–0–7531–8154–6 (hb)
ISBN 978–0–7531–8155–3 (pb)


Printed and bound in Great Britain by
T. J. International Ltd., Padstow, Cornwall

This newly discovered novel by my mother is dedicated to Olivier Rubinstein and to the two men who found it, Olivier Philipponnat and Patrick Lienhardt; but also to everyone else who has been part of this *Fire in the Blood*.

Denise Epstein

# Translator's Note

Throughout this translation of *Fire in the Blood* I have used various terms to express an important concept that recurs in the novel: the *paysan*. This French term is extremely difficult to translate: "peasant" in English has different connotations and "farmer" is too limited. The "*paysan*" is not just a farmer, but an entire rural social class, often not necessarily working class, but still not the "bourgeoisie", middle class, despite some *paysans* being quite wealthy landowners. Irène Némirovsky's vivid description of her *paysans* illustrates the multifaceted subtleties implied in the term and brings them to life for us, her readers. *Fire in the Blood* is a gem of a novel: compact, and brilliant.

I would like to dedicate this translation to the memory of Malcolm Bowie, distinguished French scholar, mentor, friend.

Sandra Smith
Cambridge, 2007

# A Note on the Text

Until recently, only a partial text of *Fire in the Blood* was thought to exist, typed up by Irène Némirovsky's husband, Michel Epstein, to whom she often passed her manuscripts for this pupose. However, Michel's typing breaks off at the words "I felt so old" (see p. 35), leaving the novel unfinished. Did Michel stop typing when Irène was arrested and deported to Auschwitz on 13 July 1942? Or perhaps even earlier in 1942, when she could no longer find a way to get her novels and short stories published?

As readers will learn from the foreword to this novel, it is likely that Némirovsky was still working on *Fire in the Blood* in 1942. We know this thanks to the work of Olivier Philipponnat and Patrick Lienhardt, who were commissioned to write a biography of Némirovsky, and who began extensive research into her archive. Two pages of the original manuscript were found to have been in the suitcase that Némirovsky's daughter, Denise Epstein, carried with her from Issy-l'Evêque when she and her sister Elisabeth fled after their mother's arrest, and which contained Némirovsky's great lost novel *Suite Française*. And as Philipponnat and Lienhardt trawled the Némirovsky archive at the Institut Mémoires de l'édition contemporaine (IMEC), they discovered, amidst papers given by Némirovsky for safe-keeping to her editor and family friend in the spring of 1942, the rest of the missing manuscript: thirty tightly packed pages of handwriting, with very few crossings out, the beginning of which corresponded to Michel's typed version.

It is an extraordinary collection of papers, which adds to our understanding of Némirovsky's oeuvre. As well as the manuscript of *Fire in the Blood*, it contains Némirovsky's working notebooks dating back to 1933, successive versions of several of her novels — including *David Golder* — as well as outlines for *Captivité*, the projected third part of *Suite Française*.

# Foreword

In 1918 the fifteen-year-old Irène Némirovsky was living in Mustamäki, the Finnish village that had become a haven to the wealthy elite of St Petersburg since revolution broke out in Russia. To relieve the boredom, Irène wrote poems.

> Little goat grazing in the mountains,
> Galya is so happy to be alive.
> The grey wolf will devour the little goat
> But Galya will devour an entire army . . .

Nearly twenty years later, in 1937, Irène Némirovsky rediscovered these lines when she came across the slim black notebook that contained her early attempts at literature. They were a verse rewriting of Alphonse Daudet's short story, "*La Chèvre de M. Seguin*", in which the goat, Blanchette, is eaten by a wolf; in Némirovsky's version, the goat gets its revenge. "If ever you read this, my daughters, how silly you will think I was!" Némirovsky wrote. "Even I think I was silly at that happy age. But it is important to respect the past. So I won't destroy a thing."

Némirovsky remained true to her word. She tore up none of the work that belonged to her adolescence — a time when she was not entirely Russian, nor French either, nor conscious of her Jewishness. She had already mined her childhood memories and writings for material in 1934, shortly after her father's death, sketching out three novels and several stories alongside diary entries in a notebook Némirovsky called the "Monster" because of its ever-increasing size. The novels were *Le Vin de solitude, Jézebel* and *Deux*, the work of a writer at the height of her powers.

But by 1937 Irène was tired. She had written a novel a year since 1928, as well as dozens of short stories; her request for French citizenship had been pending since 1935; her inheritance was being eaten up by her extravagant and neurotic mother, forcing her to publish relentlessly in order to maintain her prominent position in the literary world, and to choose magazines with a large circulation, regardless of their political allegiance. Némirovsky's husband, who worked in a bank, earned a third of what she did; they had two daughters to support: Denise, who was eight, and little Elisabeth, born on 20 March 1937.

She sometimes lost heart. Then she would stop writing: "Anxiety, sadness, a mad desire to be reassured. Yes, that's what I seek, but in vain. Only in Paradise will I find reassurance. I think of Renan's words: 'You find peace in God's heart.' To be confident and reassured, sheltering in God's heart! And yet, I love life" (5 June 1937).

For a thirty-four-year-old, youth is over. Irène knew this and the adolescent notebook she had unearthed filled her with melancholy. On 6 December 1937 she wrote a list of possible new subjects for stories, carefully numbered from 1 to 27. Several were meditations on the various stages of life, and the passing of time, in which youth and age are at odds with each other. One of them was *Fire in the Blood*, although that was not yet its title:

> New subjects and a novel. I thought about *The Young and the Old* for a novel (a play would be better). Austerity, purity of parents who were guilty when they were young. The impossibility of understanding that "fire in the blood". A good idea. Disadvantage: no clear characters.

The book grew in her mind when, during the summer of 1938, she reread Proust's *A l'ombre des jeunes filles en fleur* (*Within a Budding Grove*). Here she found Proust's "marvellous words", which seemed to express to perfection the subject that preoccupied her:

> We do not receive wisdom, we must discover it for ourselves, after a journey through the wilderness which no one else can make for us, which no one can spare us, for our wisdom is the point of view from which we come at last to regard the world. The lives that you admire, the attitudes that seem noble to you, have not been shaped by a paterfamilias or a schoolmaster, they have sprung from very different beginnings, having been influenced by everything evil or commonplace

that prevailed round about them. They represent a struggle and a victory.[1]

However, it was Némirovsky's visit to a village in Burgundy, at the end of 1937, that provided the missing setting for her novel. She had gone there to interview a nanny for baby Elisabeth. She would return to find peace from the troubles of Paris.

The first mention of Issy-l'Evêque in her notebooks occurs on 25 April 1938: "Returned from Issy l'Evêque. 4 days full of happiness. What more could I ask? Thank God for that and for hope." Here, in this rural Arcadia, were the characters she had been seeking for her novel, those taciturn people that only the French countryside can produce. "Everyone lives in his own house, on his own land, distrusts his neighbours, harvests his wheat, counts his money and doesn't give a thought to the rest of the world," says Sylvestre, the narrator of *Fire in the Blood*. "This region has something restrained yet wild about it, something affluent and yet distrustful that is reminiscent of another time, long past."

When Sylvestre describes entering the café in the village's Hôtel des Voyageurs, it is impossible not to think that we are hearing Irène Némirovsky herself, describing her own visit to the hotel of the same name in Issy-l'Evêque:

---

[1] Marcel Proust, *In Search of Lost Time*, vol. II *Within a Budding Grove*, trans. C.K. Scott Moncrieff and Terence Kilmartin, revised by D.J. Enright (London: Vintage, 2002) p. 513

I push open the door, making a little bell ring, and find myself in the dark, smoky café. A wood-burning stove glows like a red eye; mirrors reflect the marble tabletops, the billiard table, the torn leather settee and the calendar from 1919 with its picture of an Alsatian woman in white stockings standing between two soldiers [ ... ] In front of me is a mirror that frames my wrinkled face, a face so mysteriously changed over the past few years that I scarcely recognise myself.

The face in the mirror seems like an omen, yet how could Némirovsky have known that she would spend the early weeks of the Occupation in this very hotel, and begin here her final book, *Suite Française*?

From the dazzling success of her first novel, *David Golder*, to her arrest in 1942, Irène Némirovsky never appeared to be surprised by her fate. It was as if, after the Russian Revolution, nothing human, or indeed inhuman, seemed strange to her. "Of course," stressed the writer Henri de Régnier in a 1929 review of *David Golder*, "the human subject matter that Mme Némirovsky deals with is rather repugnant, but she has observed it with passionate curiosity, and she manages to communicate this curiosity to us, so we may share it. Interest is stronger than disgust." Yet Irène Némirovsky's curiosity was to prove dangerous: it drew her to things from which she should have kept her distance.

Constructed around a gradually revealed secret, *Fire in the Blood* describes, as a naturalist might describe, a predatory community of extreme cunning. Behind the pretty rural scenery, beasts lurk in the shadows, ready to pounce, and as the reader's eye becomes accustomed to the dark, we can't miss them. This "malicious intent" at the heart of village life will become the subject of *Dolce*, the second part of *Suite Française*, which describes life under Occupation in a small rural community. The village in *Dolce* bears a very close resemblance to that in *Fire in the Blood* and is undoubtedly also based on Issy-l'Evêque.

"Ah, dear friend, when something happens in life, do you ever think about the moment that caused it, the seed from which it grew? How can I explain it . . . Imagine a field being sowed, and all the promise that's contained in a grain of wheat, all the future harvests . . . Well, it's exactly the same in life." When Némirovsky puts these words into the mouth of Hélène in *Fire in the Blood*, she is transposing a Ukrainian proverb she was fond of quoting into a Burgundy setting: "All a man needs in life is one tiny grain of luck; without it, he is nothing." She could have been talking about her own life. Without the unique circumstances of her upbringing, could she have become the author of the best-selling *David Golder*? Without the all-conquering pride that consumed her, would she have been able to escape the influence of her arrogant mother, who was obsessed by money and the desire to remain eternally youthful? Without the "passionate curiosity" that Henri de Régnier immediately recognised in her, would she have been able to portray so vividly the world of the *paysans,* to evoke their work and their daily lives from so close up?

In *Fire in the Blood* the name of the village hotel and the mill remain exactly as they are in life. The real Moulin-Neuf is close to a pond, about one kilometre from Issy-l'Evêque if you take the road from the Montjeu farm. Would Némirovsky have changed the names of places and people if the novel had been published during her lifetime? Begun in 1938, *Fire in the Blood* was probably reworked during the summer of 1941 in Issy-l'Evêque itself. Némirovsky had moved there with her two daughters at the end of May 1940, shortly before the German invasion, and was staying at the Hôtel des Voyageurs. She had plenty of time to observe her characters in the flesh. On two occasions she drew a parallel in her notebook between *Fire in the Blood* and *Captivity,* the projected third section of *Suite Française,* for which a few notes have survived. It is therefore highly likely that she was still working on *Fire in the Blood* in 1942.

In Issy-l'Evêque Irène Némirovsky had discovered a French Arcadia. It was her love of its natural beauty that gives *Fire in the Blood* the incomparable scent of water and earth that Némirovsky savoured right up until those final moments she spent in the woods and fields of Burgundy: "a fresh, bitter smell that makes me feel so happy". However — and it is this theme that underlies the novel — even in Arcadia one can never be certain of the harvest. For, "who would bother sowing his fields, if he knew in advance what the harvest would bring?"

Olivier Philipponnat & Patrick Lienhardt

This is a shortened version of the preface to the French edition (Denoël, 2007)

We were drinking a light punch, the kind we had when I was young, and all sitting around the fire, my Erard cousins, their children and I. It was an autumn evening, the whole sky red above the sodden fields of turned earth. The fiery sunset promised a strong wind the next day; the crows were cawing. This large, icy house is full of draughts. They blew in from everywhere with the sharp, rich tang of autumn. My cousin Hélène and her daughter, Colette, were shivering beneath the shawls I'd lent them, cashmere shawls that had belonged to my mother. They asked how I could live in such a rat hole, just as they did every time they came to see me, and Colette, who is shortly to be married, spoke proudly of the charms of the Moulin-Neuf where she would soon be living, and "where I hope to see you often, Cousin Silvio", she said. She looked at me with pity. I am old, poor and unmarried, holed up in a farmer's hovel in the middle of the woods. Everyone knows I've travelled, that I've worked my way through my inheritance. A prodigal son. By the time I got back to the place where I was born, even the fatted calf had waited for me for so long it had died of old age. Comparing their lot with mine, the Erards no doubt forgave me for borrowing money I had never returned and repeated, after their daughter, "You live like an animal here, you poor dear. You should go and spend the summer with Colette once she's settled in."

I still have happy moments, though they don't realise it. Today, I'm alone; the first snow has fallen. This region, in the middle of France, is both wild and rich. Everyone lives in his own house, on his own land, distrusts his neighbours, harvests his wheat, counts his money and doesn't give a thought to the rest of the world. No châteaux, no visitors. A bourgeoisie reigns here that has only recently emerged from the working classes and is still very close to them, part of a rich bloodline that loves everything that has its roots in the land. My family is spread over the entire province — an extensive network of Erards, Chapelains, Benoîts, Montrifauts; they are important farmers, lawyers, government officials, landowners. Their houses are imposing and isolated, built far from the villages and protected by great forbidding doors with triple locks, like the doors you find in prisons. Their flat gardens contain almost no flowers, nothing but vegetables and fruit trees trained to produce the best yield. Their sitting rooms are stuffed full of furniture and always shut up; they live in the kitchen to save money on firewood. I'm not talking about François and Hélène Erard, of course; I have never been in a home more pleasant, welcoming, intimate, warm and happy than theirs. But, in spite of everything, my idea of the perfect evening is this: I am completely alone; my housekeeper has just put the hens in their coop and gone home, and

2

I am left with my pipe, my dog nestled between my legs, the sound of the mice in the attic, a crackling fire, no newspapers, no books, a bottle of red wine warming slowly on the hearth.

"Why do people call you Silvio?" asked Colette.

"A beautiful woman who was once in love with me thought I looked like a gondolier," I replied. "That was over twenty years ago and, at the time, I had black hair and a handlebar moustache. She changed my name from Sylvestre to Silvio."

"But you look like a faun," said Colette, "with your wide forehead, turned-up nose, pointed ears and laughing eyes. Sylvestre, creature of the woods. That suits you very well."

Of all of Hélène's children, Colette is my favourite. She isn't beautiful, but she has the quality that, when I was young, I used to value most in women: she has fire. Her eyes laugh like mine and her large mouth too; her hair is black and fine, peeping out in delicate curls from behind the shawl, which she has pulled over her head to keep the draught from her neck. People say she looks like the young Hélène. But I can't remember. Since the birth of a third son, little Loulou, who's nine years old now, Hélène has put on weight and the woman of forty-eight, whose soft skin has lost its bloom, obscures my memory of the Hélène I knew when she was twenty. She looks calm and happy now.

This gathering at my house was arranged to introduce Colette's fiancé to me. His name is Jean Dorin, one of the Dorins from the Moulin-Neuf, who've been millers for generations. A beautiful river, frothy and green, runs past their mill. I used to go trout fishing there when Dorin's father was still alive.

"You'll make us some good fish dishes, Colette," I said.

François refused a glass of punch: he drinks only water. He has a pointy little grey beard that he slowly strokes.

"You won't miss the pleasures of this world when you've left it," I remarked to him, "or rather once it has left you, as it has me . . ."

For I sometimes feel I've been rejected by life, as if washed ashore by the tide. I've ended up on a lonely beach, an old boat, still solid and seaworthy, but whose paint has faded in the water, eaten away by salt.

"No, since you don't like wine, hunting, or women, you'll have nothing to miss."

"I'd miss my wife," he replied, smiling.

That was when Colette went and sat next to her mother.

"Mama, tell me the story of how you got engaged to Papa," she said. "You've never said anything about it. Why's that? I know it's a very romantic story, that you loved each other for a long time . . . Why haven't you ever told me about it?"

"You've never asked."

"Well, I'm asking now."

Hélène laughed. "It's none of your business," she protested.

"You don't want to say because you're embarrassed. But it can't be because of Uncle Silvio: he must know all about it. Is it because of Jean? But he'll soon be your

4

son, Mama, and he should know you as well as I do. I so want Jean and me to live together the way you live with Papa. I'm positive you've never had a fight."

"It's not Jean I'm embarrassed about, but these great oafs," said Hélène, nodding towards her sons with a smile. They were sitting on the floor, throwing pine cones into the fire; they had pockets full of them; the cones burst open in the flames with a loud, crackling sound.

Georges was fifteen and Henri thirteen. "If it's because of us," they replied, "go ahead, don't be embarrassed."

"We're not interested in your love stories," Georges said scornfully. He was at that age when a boy's voice starts to change.

As for little Loulou, he'd fallen asleep.

But Hélène shook her head and was reluctant to speak.

"You have the perfect marriage," Colette's fiancé said shyly. "I hope that we too . . . one day . . ."

He was mumbling. He seemed a good lad, his face thin and soft, with the beautiful anxious eyes of a hare. Strange that Hélène and Colette, mother and daughter, should have sought out the same type of man to marry. Someone sensitive, considerate, easily dominated; almost feminine, but at the same time guarded and shy, with a kind of fierce modesty. Good Lord, I was nothing like that! Standing slightly apart, I looked at the seven of them. We'd eaten in the sitting room, which is the only habitable room in the house, except for the kitchen; I sleep in a kind of attic room under the eaves. The sitting room is always rather gloomy and, on this November evening, was so dark that when the fire was low, all you could see were the large cauldrons and antique warming pans hanging from the walls, whose copper bottoms reflected even the dimmest light. When the flames rose again, the fire lit up their calm faces, their kind smiles, Hélène's hand with its gold wedding band stroking little Loulou's curls. Hélène was wearing a blue silk dress with white polka dots. My mother's shawl, embroidered with leaves, covered her shoulders. François sat next to her; both of them looked at the children sitting at their feet. I picked up a flaming twig from the fire to relight my pipe and it illuminated my face. It seems I wasn't the only one observing what was happening around me for Colette, who doesn't miss a thing either, suddenly exclaimed, "Why, Cousin Silvio, you have such a mocking look sometimes. I've often noticed it."

Then she turned to her father. "I'm still waiting to hear all about how you fell in love, Papa."

"I'll tell you about the first time I ever met your mother," said François. "Your grandfather lived in town, then. As you know, he'd been married twice. Your mother was his child from the first marriage and her stepmother also had a daughter from her first marriage. What you don't know is that I was supposed to marry the other young lady, your mother's half-sister."

"How funny," said Colette.

"Yes, you see how chance comes into it. So I went to their house, trailing behind my parents. I was as keen on getting married as a dog is on getting whipped. But my mother, poor woman, insisted I settle down and she told me that, after a great deal of coaxing, she had managed to arrange this meeting, with no obligation, of course. We went inside. Picture the coldest, most austere sitting room in the whole province. Above the fireplace there were two bronze candelabra depicting the flames of love. I can picture them to this day . . . horrible."

"And what about me?" Hélène said, laughing. "Those frozen flames were symbolic in that sitting room where no one ever lit a fire."

"Your grandfather's second wife, well, I won't mince words, was by nature . . ."

"Don't," said Hélène, "she's dead."

"Fortunately . . . But your mother is right: the dead should rest in peace. She was a heavy woman with very pale skin who wore her red hair in a large bun. Her daughter looked like a turnip. The whole time I was there, that poor creature kept crossing and uncrossing her hands over her knees; she had chilblains on her fingers and she didn't say a word. It was winter. We were offered six biscuits out of a fruit bowl and some chocolates that were so old they'd turned white. My mother, who was sensitive to the cold, couldn't stop sneezing. I left as soon as I could. But as we were at the door, looking at the snow that had just begun to fall, I saw some children coming home from the local school. I noticed one of them, running and slipping in the snow. She was wearing big wooden clogs and a red cape; she had rosy cheeks, her black hair was all dishevelled, and there was snow on the tip of her nose

7

and on her eyelashes. She was a young girl, only thirteen. It was your mother: she was being chased by some boys who were throwing snowballs down the back of her neck. She was only a few steps away from me; she turned around, gathered up some snow and threw it straight up in the air, laughing; then, since one of her clogs was full of snow, she took it off and stood on the doorstep, hopping on one foot, her black hair flying around her face. You can't imagine how lively and attractive I found this little girl after that icy sitting room and those boring people. My mother told me who she was. It was at that very moment that I decided I would marry her. Go ahead and laugh, my darlings. What I felt was less a desire, or a wish, than a kind of vision. In my mind's eye I could picture her in the future, coming out of church by my side, as my wife . . .

"She wasn't happy. Her father was old and ill; her stepmother didn't care about her. I managed to get her invited to my parents' house. I helped her do her homework; I lent her books; I organised picnics, little outings for her, her alone. She never suspected . . ."

"Of course I did," said Hélène, and beneath her grey hair she gave a girlish smile and her eyes lit up with a mischievous gleam.

"I went away to Paris to finish my studies. You don't ask for the hand of a thirteen-year-old girl in marriage; I went off thinking I'd come back in five years and would then ask to marry her. But at seventeen she married someone else. Her husband was a very good man, much older than her. She would have married just about anyone to get away from her stepmother."

"Towards the end she was so mean", said Hélène, "that my half-sister and I only had one pair of gloves. In theory we were meant to take turns wearing them when we went out to see people. But my stepmother managed to punish me for something every time we were supposed to go somewhere, so it was her own daughter who always wore the gloves. They were beautiful kid gloves. They made me so envious I decided I would say yes to the first man who asked to marry me, even if he didn't love me, just to have a pair of my own, my very own. The young are so foolish . . ."

"I was very upset," said François, "and when I came home and saw the lovely, rather sad young woman my friend had become, I fell very much in love . . . As for her . . ." He fell silent.

"Oh, see how they're blushing," cried Colette, clapping her hands, looking back and forth between her mother and father. "Come on, now, tell all! That's when your love story started, isn't it? You spoke to each other, you had an understanding. He went away again, with a heavy heart, because you weren't free. He waited faithfully and when you were widowed, he came back and married you. You lived happily ever after and had many children."

"Yes, that's right," said Hélène, "but, my God, before that, what anxiety, what tears! Everything seemed impossible to put right. But how long ago all that was . . . When my first husband died, your father was away, travelling. I thought he'd forgotten all about me, that he was never coming back. When you're young, you're so impatient. Every day that passes, every day without your love rips you apart. Finally, he came back."

It was pitch black outside now. I got up and closed the heavy wooden shutters; their mournful creak broke the silence and made everyone jump. Hélène said it was time for them to go. Jean Dorin obediently stood up and went to get the ladies' coats from my bedroom. I heard Colette ask, "Mama, what happened to your half-sister?"

"She died, my darling. Do you remember, it was seven years ago and your father and I went to a funeral at Coudray, in the Nièvre. That was poor Cécile's funeral."

"Was she as mean as her mother?"

"Cécile? Not at all, the poor thing! You couldn't find a sweeter, nicer person. She loved me dearly and I loved her too. She was a real sister to me."

"It's odd that she never came to see us . . ."

Hélène didn't reply. Colette asked her another question; again, no reply. Colette wouldn't let it go.

"Oh, but it was all so very long ago," her mother said finally, her voice altering to become strangely distant, as if she were speaking through a dream.

Colette's fiancé came back with the coats and we all went outside. I walked my cousins back to their house. They live in a lovely house about four kilometres from here. We took a narrow, muddy road, the boys in front with their father, then Colette and Jean, with Hélène and me bringing up the rear.

Hélène talked about the young couple.

"Jean Dorin seems like a good lad, don't you think? They've known each other for a long time. They have every chance of being happy together. They'll live as François and I have, they'll be close, they'll have a dignified, peaceful life . . . yes, peaceful . . . tranquil and serene . . . Is it really so difficult to be happy? I think there's something soothing about the Moulin-Neuf. I've always dreamt of having a house near a river, waking up in the middle of the night, all warm in my bed, listening to the flowing water. Soon, they'll have a child," she continued, dreaming out loud. "My God, if only one could know at twenty how simple life is . . ."

I said goodbye to them at the garden gate; it opened with a squeak and closed again with that heavy, gong-like sound that is as pleasing to the ear as a mature bottle of Burgundy to the palate. The house is covered in thick green vines that quiver in the slightest breeze, but at that time of year only a few dry leaves were left, and the wire trellis glinted in the moonlight. After the Erards had gone inside, I stood next to Jean Dorin for a moment on the road, watching the lights go on, one after the other, in the sitting room and bedrooms; they shed a peaceful glow into the night.

"We're counting on you to come to the wedding. You will come, won't you?" Colette's fiancé asked anxiously.

"But of course! It's been a good ten years since I went to a wedding reception," I said and I could picture all the ones I'd been to, all those great rural feasts: the ruddy cheeks of the men as they drank, the young men borrowed from the neighbouring villages along with the chairs and the wooden dance floor; the Bombe Glacée for dessert and the groom in pain because his shoes are too tight; and, from every nook and cranny of the surrounding countryside, the family, friends and neighbours — people sometimes not seen in years, but who suddenly turn up, like corks bobbing to the surface, each one awakening the memory of quarrels that started back in the mists of time, past loves, former grudges, engagements broken then forgotten, inheritances and law suits . . .

Old Uncle Chapelain who married his cook, the two Montrifaut sisters, who haven't spoken to each other in fourteen years, even though they live in the same street, because one of them once refused to lend the other her special jam-making pan, and the lawyer whose wife is in Paris with a travelling salesman, and . . . My God, a wedding in the provinces is such a gathering of ghosts! In big cities, people either see each other all the time or never, it's simpler. Here . . . Corks in water, that's what I say. Hey presto, there they are! And what a stir they cause, how many old memories they dredge up. Then down they go again and, for ten years, they're forgotten.

I whistled for my dog and quickly said goodbye to Colette's fiancé. I went home. It feels good at my house, with the fire dying down: when the flames have stopped dancing, when they no longer leap in all directions sending out thousands of little sparks to shine pointlessly without providing light, warmth or benefit to anyone, when the fire is happy simply slowly to boil the kettle, that's when it feels good.

12

Colette got married on 30 November at twelve o'clock. The family gathered together for a magnificent meal followed by dancing. In the early hours of the morning I walked home through the Maie Forest. At that time of year its paths are so muddy and covered in such a thick carpet of leaves that you have to walk slowly, as if wading through a marsh. I had stayed late at the wedding. I'd been waiting: there was someone I wanted to see dance . . . Moulin-Neuf is near Coudray, where Hélène's half-sister Cécile used to live. On her death, she had left her property to her ward, a child she'd taken in and who is now married; her name is Brigitte Declos. I wasn't sure whether Coudray and the Moulin-Neuf were on friendly terms, or if I would get to see the young woman. But in fact, she did turn up.

She is tall and very beautiful, with a look of boldness, vigour and strength. She has green eyes and black hair. She is twenty-four. She was wearing a short black dress. Of all the women there, she was the only one who hadn't got dressed up to attend the wedding. I even had the impression that she had chosen simple clothes deliberately, in order to express the scorn she feels towards this mistrustful place: she's considered an outsider. Everyone knows she was adopted, no better, really, than the welfare girls who work on our farms. And to top it all she married someone who is virtually a peasant, an old, sly, stingy man who owns the best land in the area, but only speaks in the local dialect and herds his cows into the fields himself. It was clear she knew how to squander his money: her dress was from Paris and she was wearing several large diamond rings.

I know her husband well: he is the one who bought up my meagre inheritance bit by bit. I sometimes run into him on Sundays. He has changed his clogs for shoes, shaved himself and put on a cap, in order to come and contemplate the fields I've sold him, where his cattle now graze. He leans against the fence and plants the thick, knotty stick that's always with him in the ground; he rests his chin on his large, strong hands and looks out at the scene in front of him. As for me, I just pass by. I'm off for a walk with my dog, or out hunting. When I return home at dusk he's still there; he hasn't budged; he's been thinking about what he owns; he's happy. His young wife never comes near my land. I had been eager to see her and had tried to find out about her from Jean Dorin.

"Do you know her, then?" he asked. "We're neighbours and her husband is one of my clients. I'll invite them to the wedding and we'll be obliged to see them socially, but I don't want her getting friendly with Colette. I don't like her behaviour when it comes to men."

When the young woman came in, Hélène was standing not far from me. She was nervous and tired.

14

The meal was over. A hundred people had been served lunch at tables arranged on a special wooden floor brought in from Moulins for the dance and set up under a marquee. It wasn't too cold out, the weather damp but fine. Every now and again, one of the canvas tent-flaps would fly up and you could see the Erards' large garden, the bare trees, the pond covered in dead leaves. At five o'clock the tables were taken away and the dancing began. Some more guests arrived; they were the youngest, the ones more interested in dancing than food; it's rare to have any entertainment in these parts. Brigitte Declos was among them, but she didn't seem to know anyone very well. She was alone. Hélène shook her hand, as she did with everyone; but for a moment her lips tightened into a weak, brave smile — the kind that women use to hide their most secret thoughts.

The older people made way for the youngsters in the improvised ballroom and went into the house. We sat in a circle around the large fireplaces; it was stiflingly hot in those stuffy rooms; we drank grenadine and punch. The men talked about the harvest, the farms rented out to tenants, the price of cattle. When older people get together there is something unflappable about them; you can sense they've tasted all the heavy, bitter, spicy food of life, extracted its poisons, and will now spend ten or fifteen years in a state of perfect equilibrium and enviable morality. They are happy with themselves. They have renounced the vain attempts of youth to adapt the world to their desires. They have failed and, now, they can relax. In a few years they will once again

15

be troubled by great anxiety, but this time it will be a fear of death; it will have a strange effect on their tastes, it will make them indifferent, or eccentric, or moody, incomprehensible to their families, strangers to their children. But between the ages of forty and sixty they enjoy a precarious sense of tranquillity.

I felt this all the more strongly after such a good meal and excellent wine, thinking back to the past and the cruel enemy who made me run away from this place. I tried being a civil servant in the Congo, a merchant in Tahiti, a trapper in Canada. Nothing made me happy. I thought I was seeking my fortune; in reality I was being propelled forward by the fire in my young blood. But as these passions are now extinguished I no longer know who I am. I feel I've travelled a long, pointless road, simply to end up where I began. The only thing I am truly happy about is that I never married. But I shouldn't have roamed all over the world. I should have stayed here and looked after my land; I'd be wealthier today. I'd be the rich uncle. I could take my rightful place in society instead of wandering among these sturdy, calm people like a breeze blowing through the trees.

I decided to go and watch the young people dance. You could see the outline of the enormous marquee in the darkness; you could hear the music of the orchestra. The strings of electric light bulbs that had been rigged up inside cast the dancers' shadows on to the canvas. It's the same tent for Bastille Day and country fairs; that's how things are done here . . . The wind was whispering in the autumn trees and every now and

**16**

again the marquee seemed to sway, like a ship. And so this sight, seen through the darkness, seemed strange and sad. I don't know why. Perhaps because of the contrast between the stillness of nature and the turbulence of youth. Poor children! They threw themselves into it all with such pleasure. The young girls especially: they're raised so strictly and puritanically around here. Boarding school in Moulins or Nevers until they're eighteen, then lessons in running a household, under the everwatchful eyes of their mothers, until they get married. Their bodies and souls are bursting with energy, vitality, desire . . .

I went into the marquee and watched them; I listened to their laughter. I wondered how they could get such enjoyment from prancing around in time to the music. For some time now, when I'm with young people, I feel a kind of astonishment, as if I'm looking at a species utterly different from mine, the way an old dog watches the comings and goings of little mice. I asked Hélène and François if they ever felt anything similar. They laughed and said I was nothing but an old egotist, that they weren't losing contact with their children, thank God. So that's what they believe! I think they're deluding themselves. If they could see their own youth resurrected before them, it would horrify them, or else they wouldn't recognise it; they would stare at it and say, "That love, those dreams, that fire are strangers to us." Their own youth . . . So how can they possibly expect to understand anyone else's?

While the orchestra was having a break, I heard the carriage set off, taking the newlyweds to the

Moulin-Neuf. I looked for Brigitte Declos in the crowd. She was dancing with a tall dark young man. I thought of her husband — such a fool. Then again, maybe he was wise, in his own way. He kept his old body snug under a red eiderdown and his old soul warm at the thought of all the land he owned, while his wife enjoyed her youth.

I always have lunch with the Erards on New Year's Day. The tradition is that you stay a long time. You arrive around noon, spend all afternoon with them, dine off the leftovers from lunch, then go home late in the evening. François had to visit one of his properties. Winter is harsh; the roads are covered in snow. He left around five o'clock. At eight o'clock we were still waiting for him, to have supper, but he was nowhere in sight.

"He must have been delayed," I said. "He'll spend the night at the farm."

"No, he knows I'm waiting for him," Hélène replied. "Not once in all the time we've been married has he stayed away overnight without telling me. Let's eat; he'll be home soon."

The three boys were at the Moulin-Neuf where their sister had invited them to spend the night. It had been a long time since Hélène and I had been alone together like this. We talked about the weather, the harvest, the only real topics of conversation in these parts; we had a relaxing meal. This region has something restrained yet wild about it, something affluent and yet distrustful that is reminiscent of another time, long past.

The dining-room table seemed too big for just the two of us. Everything sparkled; everything gave off the feeling of respectability and calm: the oak furniture, the gleaming parquet floors, the plates decorated with flowers, the enormous sideboard with its curved silhouette, the kind that, nowadays, you can only find around here, the clock, the bronze ornaments on the hearth, the lamp hanging down from the ceiling and the little hatch cut into the oak wall that opens into the kitchen so the dishes can be passed through. What a magnificent household my cousin Hélène runs. How expert she is at jam-making, preserves, pastry. How well she tends her hens and her garden. I asked if she had managed to save the twelve little rabbits whose mother had died and whom she'd nursed with a baby's bottle.

"They're doing wonderfully," she replied.

But I could sense she was preoccupied. She kept glancing at the clock and straining to hear the sound of the car.

"You're worried about François, aren't you? I can tell. What could possibly have happened to him?"

"Nothing. But, you see, François and I are rarely ever apart; we're so close that I suffer when he isn't here beside me, I worry. I know it's silly . . ."

"You were apart during the war . . ."

"Oh," she said and shuddered at the memory. "Those five years were so hard, so terrible . . . I sometimes think they overshadow all the rest."

We both fell silent; the little hatch creaked open and the maid passed us a fruit tart, made from the last apples of winter. The clock struck nine.

"Monsieur has never been this late," said the maid from inside the kitchen.

It was snowing. Neither of us said anything. Colette phoned from the Moulin-Neuf; everything was fine there.

"When are you going to go and visit Colette?" Hélène reproached me for my laziness.

"It's far," I replied.

"You old owl . . . No one can lure you out of your nest. To think there was a time when . . . When I think about how you used to live among natives, Lord knows where . . . and now, to go to Mont-Tharaud or the Moulin-Neuf, *it's far*," she repeated, mocking me. "You must see them, Sylvestre. Those dear children are so happy. Colette looks after the farm; they have a model dairy. When she lived here she was a bit listless, she pampered herself. Now that she has her own house she's the first one up, pitching in, taking care of everything. Dorin's father completely renovated the Moulin-Neuf before he died. Naturally, it's out of the question to sell it: the mill has been in his family for a hundred and fifty years. They can take things slowly; they have everything they need to be happy: work and youth."

She continued talking about them, imagining the future and already picturing Colette's children. Outside, the great cedar tree heavy with snow creaked and groaned. At nine thirty, she suddenly stopped talking.

Then she said, "This is very strange. He should have been home by seven o'clock."

She wasn't hungry any more; she pushed her plate away and we waited in silence. But the evening passed and still he wasn't home.

Hélène looked up at me. "When a woman loves her husband as I love François, she shouldn't outlive him. He's older than me and not as strong . . . Sometimes, I'm afraid."

She threw a log on to the fire.

"Ah, dear friend, when something happens in life, do you ever think about the moment that caused it, the seed from which it grew? How can I explain it . . . Imagine a field being sowed and all the promise that's contained in a grain of wheat, all the future harvests . . . Well, it's exactly the same in life. When I saw François for the very first time, the instant we looked into each other's eyes, so much happened in that moment . . . it makes me feel faint to think of it. Our love, our separation, those three years he spent in Dakar, when I was someone else's wife, and . . . everything else . . . Then the war, the children . . . Happy things, but sad things as well, the idea that he could die, or *I* might, and the desperate unhappiness of the one left behind."

"Yes," I said, "but who would bother sowing his fields if he knew in advance what the harvest would bring?"

"But everyone would, Silvio," she replied, calling me by the name she hardly ever used now. "That's what life is all about, joy and tears. Everyone wants to live life, everyone except you."

22

I looked at her and smiled. "You love François so much."

"I love him very much," she said simply.

Someone knocked on the kitchen door. It was a young lad who'd borrowed a crate for some chickens the day before and was returning it to the maid. Through the half-open window I heard his loud voice: "Been an accident near the lake at Buire."

"What kind of accident?" the cook asked.

"Car got itself smashed to bits on the road and someone got hurt. They took him to Buire."

"Do you know his name?"

"No, dunno," said the boy.

"It's François," said Hélène, who'd gone white.

"Come on, that's mad!"

"I just know it's François."

"He would have phoned if he'd had an accident."

"But you know what he's like, don't you? To spare me getting upset and going over to Buire in the dark, he's going to try and get himself brought back here, even if he's injured or dying."

"But he'll never find a car at this time of night, in the snow."

She walked out of the dining room and got her coat and shawl from the entrance hall.

"That's mad," was all I could say again. "You don't even know for sure it was François in that accident. And, anyway, how are you going to get to Buire?"

"Well . . . I'll walk, if I have no other choice."

"Eleven kilometres!"

She didn't even reply. I tried to borrow a car from the neighbours. No luck: one had broken down, the other belonged to the doctor, who needed it to drive a patient to the next town for an operation. Bicycles were useless in the thick snow. We had no choice but to walk. It was extremely cold. Hélène walked quickly, in silence: she was certain that François was at Buire. I didn't try to talk her out of it. I thought she was definitely capable of hearing her injured husband calling out to her. There is a kind of superhuman power in conjugal love. As the Church says, it's a great mystery. Many other things are mysteries in love as well.

Occasionally we came across a car crawling along the road in the snow. Hélène looked anxiously inside and shouted "François!" but no one answered. She didn't seem tired. She walked on, undaunted, striding along the icy road, in the dead of night, between two banks of snow, without stumbling or losing her footing a single time. I wondered what her face would look like if we got to Buire and François wasn't there.

But she wasn't wrong. It was indeed his car that had crashed near the lake. In the farmhouse, stretched out on a large bed near the fire, we found François, with a broken leg and burning with fever. When we came in he let out a weak cry of joy. "Oh, Hélène . . . Why? You shouldn't have come . . . We were going to wait for a horse and cart to take me back home. It was very silly of you to come," he said again.

But as she uncovered his leg and began to dress it with her skilful, gentle touch (she'd been a nurse

24

during the war), I saw him take her hand. "I knew you'd come," he whispered. "I was in pain and I was calling out your name."

François had to stay in bed all winter; his leg was broken in two places. There were complications, I'm not sure of the details . . . He's only been up and about for a week now.

We've had a very cold summer and not much fruit. Nothing new has happened locally. My cousin Colette Dorin gave birth on 20 September. A boy. I'd only been to the Moulin-Neuf once since their wedding. I went again when the child was born. Hélène was with her daughter. Now it's winter again — a monotonous time of year. The oriental proverb that says "the days drag on while the years fly by" is truer here than anywhere else. Once again, darkness falls at three o'clock, the crows circle the skies, there's snow on the roads and, in each isolated house, life closes in on itself even more, or so it seems — the space it offers to the outside world grows even smaller: long hours spent sitting by the fire doing nothing, not reading, not drinking, not even dreaming.

Yesterday, on 1 March, a day of sun and high wind, I left my house early to go to Coudray. Old Declos has purchased one of my fields and owes me eight thousand francs. I got held up in the village, where someone bought me a bottle of wine. When I got to Coudray it was dusk. I crossed a small wood. You could see its young, delicate trees from the road; they separate Coudray from the Moulin-Neuf. The sun was setting. As I walked through the wood, the trees were casting shadows on the ground, and it already felt like night. I love our silent woods. You never meet a soul ordinarily. So I was surprised to hear, all of a sudden, a woman's voice calling out, quite close to me. A high-pitched call, on two notes. Someone whistled in reply. The voice fell silent. I was near the small lake by then. The woods in these parts have many little lakes; you can't see them because they're surrounded by trees and hidden by rows of rushes. But I know them all. During the hunting season I spend all day on their banks.

I moved softly. The water shimmered, giving off a pale light, like a mirror in a dark room. I saw a man and a woman walk towards each other along a path between the rushes. I couldn't see their faces, only the shapes of their bodies (they were both tall and well built); the woman was wearing a red jacket. I continued on my way; they didn't see me; they were kissing.

When I arrived at Declos's house he was alone, dozing in a large armchair beside the open window. He opened his eyes, let out a deep, furious sigh and stared at me for a long time without recognising me.

I asked him if he was ill. But he's a true farmer: illness is shameful and must be concealed until the last possible moment, until death is seeping from your pores. He replied he was in excellent health, but the yellowish colour of his skin, the purple circles around his eyes, the folds in his clothing that hung loose from his body, his shortness of breath, his weakness, all betrayed him. I've heard people say he's got "a bad tumour". It must be true. Brigitte will soon find herself a rich widow.

"Where's your wife?" I asked.

"My wife, you say?"

He has the old habit of a horse trader (which he was when he was younger) of pretending to be deaf. He ended up mumbling something about his wife being at the Moulin-Neuf, at Colette Dorin's place. "She's got nothing to do, that one, except stroll about and go to see people all day long," he concluded bitterly.

That was how I learned that the two women were friends, something that Hélène certainly didn't know, for she had assured me a few days before that Colette lived only for her husband, her child, her home and refused any invitations to go out.

Old Declos gestured to me to have a seat. He's so stingy that it pains him to have to offer anyone something to drink and I took malicious pleasure in asking him for a glass of wine so I could drink to his health.

"Can't hear you," he muttered. "I have a terrible buzzing in my ear: it's from the wind."

I mentioned the money he owes me. He sighed, pulled a big key out of his pocket and pushed his chair over to the cupboard. But the drawer he wanted to open was much too high; he made several vain attempts to reach it, refused to give me the key when I asked for it and finally said that his wife would surely be home soon and would pay me.

"You have a beautiful young wife, Declos."

"Too young for my old carcass, is that what you think, Monsieur Sylvestre? Well, if she finds the nights long, at least the days pass quickly."

At that moment Brigitte came in. She was wearing a black skirt and a red jacket, and there was a young man with her: the same one who had danced with her at Colette's wedding. In my mind I finished the old man's sentence: "Quicker than you might think, Declos."

But the old man didn't seem like a fool. He looked at his wife, and his half-dead face lit up with passion and anger. "Well, finally! I've been waiting for you since midday."

She shook my hand and introduced the young man who was with her. He's called Marc Ohnet; he lives on his father's land. He has a reputation for getting into fights and for being a womaniser. He's very handsome.

I hadn't realised that Brigitte Declos and Marc Ohnet "stepped out together", as the locals say. But around here, malicious gossip stops at the edge of town; in the countryside, in these isolated houses separated by fields and deep woods, many things happen that no one knows about. As for me, well, even if I hadn't seen that red jacket near the lake an hour before, I would have guessed that these young people were in love: their calm, arrogant demeanour, and a kind of stifled passion concealed in their movements, in their smiles, gave them away. Especially her. She was *burning*. "She finds the nights long," old Declos had said. I could picture those nights, nights in her old husband's bed, dreaming of her lover, counting her husband's sighs, wondering, "When will he finally stop breathing?"

She opened the cupboard, which I imagined to be stuffed full of money beneath piles of sheets; this isn't the kind of place where we make bankers even richer; everyone keeps his possessions close, like a cherished child. I glanced at Marc Ohnet to see if I could catch a glimmer of envy on his face, for no one's rich in his family: his father was the eldest of fourteen children and his share of the property is small. But no. As soon as he saw the money he quickly turned away. He went over to the window and stared out of it for a long time: you could see the valley and the woods in the clear night. It was the kind of March weather when the wind seems to chase every single speck of cloud and fog from the sky; the stars sparkled brightly above.

"How's Colette?" I asked. "Did you see her today?"
"She's fine."

"And her husband?"

"Her husband's away. He's in Nevers and won't get back until tomorrow."

She answered my questions but never took her eyes off the tall, dark young man's face. His whole being looks supple and strong, not exactly brutal, but a bit wild; his hair is black, his forehead narrow, his teeth white, close together and rather sharp. He brought to this dismal room the smell of the woods in spring, a sharp, invigorating smell that brings life to my old bones. I could have gone on walking all night. When I left Coudray the idea of going home was unbearable, so I headed towards the Moulin-Neuf where I would ask to have supper. I crossed the wood; it was totally deserted this time, mysterious in the whistling wind.

I walked towards the river; I had only ever been to the mill in daylight before, when it was working. The noise of the wheel turning — powerful but gentle at the same time — soothes the heart. Now, the silence felt strange to me. It made me almost uncomfortable. You strained to hear each sound, in spite of yourself; but there was nothing except the rush of water. I went over the footbridge; here you are hit by a cold smell: the water, the darkness, the damp reeds. The night was so clear that you could see the white foam on the fast-flowing stream. There was a light on upstairs: Colette waiting for her husband. The wooden boards creaked beneath my feet; she heard me coming. The door opened and I could see Colette running towards me, but when she was a few steps away from me she stopped.

"Who's there?" she asked, her voice faltering.

I said my name. "You were expecting Jean, I suppose?" I continued.

She didn't reply. She walked slowly towards me so I could kiss her forehead. She wasn't wearing a hat and was dressed in a light dressing gown, as if she had just got out of bed. Her forehead was burning hot; her entire manner seemed so peculiar that I suddenly wondered what was going on.

"Am I disturbing you? I thought I would ask for some supper."

"Well . . . I'd be very happy to," she murmured, "but, it's just that I wasn't expecting you, and . . . I'm not feeling well . . . Jean's away . . . I sent the maid home and had some milk for my supper, in bed."

The longer she spoke, the more confident she became. She ended up telling me a very plausible little story: she had a touch of flu . . . if I touched her hands and cheeks, I'd see she had a fever; the maid was in the village, at her daughter's house, and wouldn't be back until the next day. She was very sorry not to be able to offer me a proper supper, but if I would be happy with some fried eggs and fruit . . . Nevertheless, she made no move to invite me inside. Quite the opposite. She blocked the door and, when I got closer to her, I could sense she was shaking all over. I felt sorry for her.

"Fried eggs won't do," I said, "I'm hungry. And besides, I don't want to keep you out on this footbridge; the wind is freezing cold. Go back to bed, my girl. I'll come some other time."

What else could I do? I'm neither her father nor her husband. Besides, to tell the truth, I don't have the right to criticise, having committed enough folly in my own youth. And aren't the most beautiful follies the ones linked to love? Quite apart from the fact that we usually pay so dearly for our follies, we should be generous about them, to ourselves and others. Yes, we always pay for them, and sometimes the smallest indiscretions cost as much as the largest. Might as well be hanged for a sheep as a lamb. Of course, it was madness to have another man in your husband's house, but on the other hand what pleasure, on a night like this, to walk arm in arm with your lover while the water flows by and the fear of being caught clutches at your heart. Who was the man she was expecting?

"At Coudray, old Declos will gladly give me a glass of wine and a piece of cheese," I thought to myself. "And if that young man isn't there any more, there's a good chance that he's the lover in both places. He's a handsome fellow. Declos is old and as for Jean, poor Jean, even on his wedding day he looked like a man who could easily be deceived. Some people are born like that; no way around it."

Colette wanted to walk me to the wood. Every now and again she stumbled on a stone and held my arm tighter. I touched her hand; it was frozen.

"Go back home," I said. "Go on, you'll make yourself worse."

"You're not angry?" she asked.

She didn't wait for me to answer. "When you see Mama," she said quietly, "I beg you, please don't say anything to her. She'll think I'm seriously ill and she'll worry."

"I won't even mention I've seen you."

She threw herself into my arms. "I love you so much Uncle Silvio! You understand everything."

It was almost a confession and I felt it was my duty to warn her about the dangers. But as soon as I said the words "your husband, your child, your home", she leapt back.

"I know! Don't you think I know?" she cried, and you could hear the suffering and hatred in her voice. "But I don't love my husband. I love someone else. Leave us in peace! It's nobody else's business," she said with difficulty, and she ran away so quickly that I didn't have time to finish what I'd started to say. Such madness! When you're twenty love is like a fever, it makes you almost delirious. When it's over you can hardly remember how it happened ... Fire in the blood, how quickly it burns itself out. Faced with this blaze of dreams and desires, I felt so old, so cold, so wise ...

At Coudray I knocked on the dining-room window and said I'd got lost. The old man couldn't refuse me a room for the night, even though he knows I've wandered around these woods since I was a child. As for dinner, I didn't stand on ceremony. I went into the kitchen and asked the maid for a bowl of soup. She gave me a large hunk of cheese and some crusty bread to go with it. I took it back to the fire to eat. There was no light in the room apart from the flames in the hearth — to save on electricity.

35

I asked where Marc Ohnet was.

"Gone."

"Did he have supper with you?"

"Yes," the old man grumbled.

"Do you see him often?"

He pretended not to hear. His wife was holding some embroidery, but she wasn't working on it. He barked at her, "Don't tire yourself out, now."

"I can't sew when there's no light," she replied, her voice quiet and distracted.

"Was anyone home at the Moulin-Neuf?" she asked, turning towards me.

"I don't know. I didn't go there. It was so dark in the woods that I never made it out. I was afraid of falling into the lake."

"Is there a lake in the woods?" she murmured and, as I was looking at her, a smile played on her lips, a mocking smile of secret joy. Then she threw her embroidery down on the table and sat very still, her hands crossed over her knees, her head lowered.

The maid came in. "I've made up Monsieur's bed," she said to me.

It seemed old Declos had fallen asleep; for a long time he sat without speaking, without moving, his mouth hanging open; his hollow cheeks and pallid skin made him look like a corpse.

"I've lit a fire in your room," the maid continued. "The nights are cold."

She broke off: Brigitte had leapt up and seemed extraordinarily perturbed. We looked at her, confused.

"Didn't you hear that?" she asked after a moment.

36

"No. What's wrong?"

"I don't know . . . I just . . . I must have been wrong . . . I thought I heard someone cry out."

I listened, but there was nothing, nothing but the almost oppressive silence of our countryside at night; even the wind had died down.

"I can't hear a thing," I said.

The maid went out. I didn't go up to bed; I was watching Brigitte. She was trembling and had gone over to the fire.

She noticed I was staring at her. "Yes," she said blankly, "the nights are very cold." She stretched out her hands as if she wanted to warm them at the fire; then, clearly forgetting I was there, she buried her face in her hands.

At that moment the garden gate creaked; someone came up to the door and rang the bell. I went to answer it; I saw one of the young farmhands standing there. It's always boys like this who bring bad news in these parts; only the wealthier people have telephones. If someone's ill, or there's been an accident or somebody's died, the farmers send one of their workers, a young lad with rosy cheeks who calmly breaks the news.

This one politely took off his cap and turned towards Brigitte. "Beg your pardon, Madame, the owner of the Moulin-Neuf fell into the river."

He answered our questions: Jean Dorin had come home from Nevers sooner than expected; he'd left his car away from the house, in the meadow; maybe he didn't want the noise from the car to disturb his wife because she was ill? While crossing the footbridge he must have felt faint; the footbridge is wide and solid, but it only has a protective handrail on one side; he'd fallen into the water. His wife hadn't heard him come home; she was asleep, but had been woken by his cry. She'd got up straight away, rushed outside and looked for him in the deep water, but without success; he must have been pulled under in a flash. She'd recognised the car standing in the meadow and was certain that her husband had just died. She was beside herself, so she'd run over to the next farm and asked for help. The men were looking for the body now, "but the farmer's mother thought that the poor lady could use some company and that Madame Declos, being her friend, would want to come," the lad concluded.

"I'll go," said Brigitte.

She seemed dumbstruck; her voice was cold and solemn. Gently, she touched her husband's shoulder, for the sound of our voices hadn't woken him. When he opened his eyes she explained what had happened. He listened in silence. Perhaps he only half understood, perhaps he cared little about the death of a young man, or even the death of anyone except himself. Perhaps he just didn't want to say what he thought. He stood up. "All this . . . all this . . ." he finally said, heaving a sigh. He didn't finish. "Well, *I'm* going to bed."

As he was leaving the room he said it again, to his wife, but in a way that struck me as significant and almost threatening: "All this is your business. Don't you get me involved, you hear?"

I walked Brigitte to the Moulin-Neuf. Flashlights shone in the dark and on the water, coming and going, criss-crossing each other as men looked for the body. At the house, all the doors were open. Some of the neighbours were tending to Colette, who'd fainted, and the baby, who was crying; others were rummaging through the cupboards, pulling out sheets they could use to wrap up the body when it was found. The farmhands were in the kitchen having a bite to eat while waiting for daylight, when they could search the reed beds further down the river; they thought the drowned man must have floated downstream and got trapped there.

I saw Colette only briefly: she was surrounded by women who evidently weren't going to leave soon. Countrywomen are never ones to miss a free show, the kind you get with a birth or sudden death. They were buzzing about, giving their advice and opinions, taking drinks to the men who were waist-high in water. I wandered around the mill, through the living quarters, so spacious and comfortable, with their large fireplaces, their pretty antique furniture, lovingly chosen by Hélène, their deep alcoves, their flowers, their floral curtains of heavy cotton; the mill itself was to the left, the domain of the absent young man. I imagined his body imprisoned in the water. But if even a small part of his soul returned to earth, it would surely come back to this humble setting, to this machinery, these sacks of grain, these weighing scales. He'd been so very proud when he'd showed me this wing of the mill, restored by his father. I almost thought I could see him standing next to me. I knocked into a piece of machinery as I passed by and suddenly it creaked, in a way that sounded so plaintive, so unexpected, so strange, that I couldn't help but whisper, "Are you here, my poor boy?"

Everything suddenly fell silent. I went back down into the living area to wait for François and Hélène; I'd had someone go and fetch them. When they arrived, their very presence restored peace almost immediately. The noise and confusion were replaced by a sort of mournful, respectful whisper. The neighbours were sent home with kind words. The windows and shutters were closed, the lights dimmed; flowers were placed in the room where the body would lie. Towards dawn, the men had found him caught in the reeds, just as they had thought; the silent little group came into the mill carrying a stretcher, and on it a body wrapped in a sheet.

Jean Dorin was buried the day before yesterday. It was a very long service on a cold and rainy afternoon. The mill is up for sale. Colette is keeping only the land; her father will look after it and she will go home to live with her parents.

A mass was said today for the repose of Jean Dorin's soul. The whole family was there, filling the church — a crowd of indifferent, silent people dressed in black. Colette has been very ill. This was her first day out of bed and during the service she fainted. I was sitting quite close to her. I saw her suddenly raise her veil and stare intently above her at the large Christ nailed to the Cross; then she let out a low moan and fell forward, her head resting on her arms. I had lunch at her parents' house after the service; she didn't come down to the dining room. I asked if I could see her; she was in her room, on the bed, her child sleeping beside her. We were alone. When she saw me she started to cry, but she refused to answer any of my questions. She just turned away with a look of shame and despair.

I finally left her alone. François and Hélène were walking slowly around the garden, waiting for me. They have aged a lot, and have lost that look of serenity that I liked so much and found so touching. I don't know whether people make their own lives, but what is certain is that the life you live ends up transforming you: a calm, happy existence gives the face a gentleness and dignity, a warm, soft look that is almost a kind of sheen, like the varnish on a painting. But now the smoothness and decorum of their features had vanished and you could see their sad, anxious souls peering through the surface. Those poor people! In nature, there is a moment of perfection when every hope is realised, when the luscious fruits finally fall, a crowning moment towards the end of summer. But it quickly passes and the autumn rains begin. It's the same for people.

My cousins were very worried about Colette. Of course they understood how very affected she was by poor Jean's death, but they had hoped she'd recover more quickly.

Quite the opposite: each day she seemed to grow weaker.

"I don't think," said François, sounding worried, "I don't think she should stay here. Not only because of all the memories she has, quite naturally, everywhere she turns — the house where she met Jean, where she got married, etc. — but because of us."

"I don't know what you mean, my dear," said Hélène, sounding agitated.

He placed his hand on her arm; he has an affectionate air of authority she can never resist.

"I think," he said, "that the sight of us, of our life, of everything that is good in our relationship intensifies her regret. She understands what she has lost more clearly; she feels it even more, so to speak, when she sees us together. Poor little thing. Sometimes she looks so sad that I can hardly bear it. She's always been my favourite, I admit it. I tried to convince her to go away, to travel. But she wouldn't. She refuses to leave us. She doesn't want to see anyone."

"I don't think she needs that kind of thing at the moment," Hélène broke in. "And even if she did, she wouldn't agree. What she needs is something serious to concentrate on. I'm sorry she's decided to sell the mill. It would have been her son's inheritance. She shouldn't just have kept it going, she should have expanded it."

"How can you say that? She wouldn't have been able to manage that all alone."

"Why all alone? We would have helped her and, in a few years, one of her brothers could have run it, until her son was old enough to take over. Some intense work is the only way she'll get better."

"Or someone else to love," I said.

"Someone else to love, of course. But the way to find him (I mean a true, sincere love) is not to think about it too much, not to yearn for him. Otherwise you make the wrong choice. You imagine you see love in the first and most ordinary face you come across. I hope with all my heart that one day, later on, she'll remarry, but first she must find peace again. Then, of course since she's young, she'll find another love, some good man like poor Jean."

They continued to talk to one another about Colette. They spoke with an air of tranquil, confident certainty. She was their child. They had made her. They thought they knew her every thought and dream. In the end they decided to do everything they could to get her interested in her estates, the farming, the harvests, all the possessions she had a duty to preserve for her son.

44

When I said goodbye to them they were sitting on a bench in front of the house, under their bedroom window, the same bench on which I had once sat for so long, listening for the sound of footsteps in the night.

Old Declos is worse. His wife called for a doctor to come from Creusot; he suggested an operation. The old man wanted to know how much it would cost and the doctor told him. Declos then sat for a long time without saying a word, just as he did that day at my house when we negotiated a price for the small estate I owned at Les Roches, after my mother died. I remember he asked my price, then went quiet for a few moments, his eyes closed; finally he said, "Agreed." He was poor back then; we were approximately the same age. It was a serious thing for him to buy twenty-four hectares of land. In the same way, when the doctor told him the operation would cost ten thousand francs and that, if it were successful he could expect to live three, four, maybe five years longer, he undoubtedly calculated the value of each of those years and decided that, in the end, they wouldn't be sufficiently pleasant or happy to justify the cost. He refused the operation; when the doctor left, he told his wife that his father had died of a similar illness, that it hadn't taken long, a few months at most, but that he'd suffered a lot.

"It doesn't matter," he concluded. "I'm used to suffering."

46

It's true: the people around here have a kind of genius for living in the most difficult way possible. No matter how rich they are, they refuse pleasure, even happiness, with implacable determination, wary perhaps of its deceptive promise. To the best of my knowledge, the only time old Declos broke this rule was the day he married Brigitte, and he must have regretted it. So he is putting his affairs in order and preparing to die at Christmas. His wife will inherit everything, there's no doubt about that. Even if he knows she's cheating on him, he'll make very sure to behave in such a way that no one else suspects her adultery. It's both a matter of pride and loyalty to the family; a kind of solidarity that ties husband and wife, father and son. In order to avoid scandal, to make sure no one knows anything, all hatreds are hidden. It's not that they seek approval: they're too primitive for that and too proud. What they fear most of all is that others might know their business. To feel judgemental eyes upon them is unbearable suffering. That's what makes them incapable of vanity: they do not wish to be envied any more than they wish others to feel sorry for them. They just want to be left in peace. Peace, that's how they put it. To them, peace is synonymous with happiness, or rather, it replaces the happiness they lack.

I heard an old woman talking to Hélène about Colette and the accident that left her a widow: "It's a shame, a real shame . . . Your daughter was at peace at the mill." And that word symbolised everything she could possibly imagine about human happiness.

47

Old Declos as well, he wants everything to be peaceful during his last days on earth, and after he's gone too.

Autumn has come early. I get up before dawn and walk through the countryside, between the fields that belonged to my family for generations, which are now owned and cultivated by others. I can't say the idea is painful to me; I have just a little twinge of sadness sometimes . . . I don't regret the time I lost trying to make my fortune, the time I bought horses in Canada, or sold cocoa beans on the Pacific coast. The need to travel, the suffocating boredom I felt in this place when I was twenty, burned within me so strongly that I think I would have died if I'd been forced to stay. My father had passed away and my mother couldn't hold me back. "It's like an illness," she said, horrified, when I begged her to give me some money and let me go. "Wait a bit and it will pass." Or "You're acting just like the Gonin boy and the Charles boy. They want to go and work in town even though they know they won't be as happy as they are here. But when I try to reason with them, all they say is 'It will make a change'."

In fact, that was exactly what I wanted: a change. My blood burned at the thought of the vast world that existed, while I simply remained here. So I left, and now I cannot understand the demon that drove me far from my home, I who am so unsociable and sedentary. I remember how Colette Dorin once told me I resembled a faun: an old faun, now, who has stopped chasing after nymphs and who huddles near the fireplace. And how can I describe the pleasure I find here? I enjoy simple things, things within reach: a nice meal, some good wine, the secret, bitter pleasure of writing in this notebook; but, most especially, this divine solitude. What else do I need? But when I was twenty, how I burned! How is this fire lit within us? It devours everything and then, in a few years, a few months, a few hours even, it burns itself out. Then you see how much damage has been done. You find yourself tied to a woman you don't love any more; or ruined, like me. Perhaps, born to be a grocer, you struggle to become a painter in Paris and end up in a hospital. Who hasn't had his life strangely warped and distorted by that fire so opposite to his true nature? Are we not all somewhat like these branches burning in my fireplace, buckling beneath the power of the flames? I'm undoubtedly wrong to generalise; there are people who are sensible at twenty, but I'll take the recklessness of my youth over their restraint any day.

I've heard that Colette will follow her father's wishes and look after her estate herself. She will be, according to François Erard, "her own manager". This will force her to see people, to go out, to fight sometimes in order to defend her son's interests. In an attempt to convince her, Hélène is using the skilful, affectionate persuasiveness she uses on little Loulou when she takes his toys away from him so he can learn his lessons. It's the same for Colette . . . Playtime is over.

Old Declos has died. He never made it to Christmas. He missed it by just a few weeks. His heart stopped. His wife is rich now. When kind Cécile, who brought her up, passed away, all Brigitte had to her name was Coudray. That is to say, nothing. The house was falling to pieces; the land had been sold. Old Declos bought Coudray; that's when he fell in love with Brigitte. Little by little he restored the farm; he knocked down the old living quarters and built the most beautiful house in the region; and, to cap it all, he married the young woman. At the time we thought how lucky she was, but I expect she would have said that Colette was more fortunate. Colette didn't have to marry an old man to be happy and pampered. But death has made them equal. I wonder if these two children know . . . or suspect . . . I doubt it: the young are concerned only with themselves. What are we to them? Fading shadows. And what are they to us?

At this time of year, when it rains every day, I go down to the village on Sundays. I pass close by the Erards' house without calling in. Sometimes, from outside the sitting-room window, you can hear Hélène playing the piano. Other times I can see her in her clogs in the garden, picking the last of the roses, the ones people save to place on graves on All Saints' Day, or wild, fire-coloured dahlias. She sees me and waves; walks over to the fence and tells me to come in. But I say no; I haven't been feeling at all sociable lately. Hélène and her family have the same effect on me as dessert wine: Muscat or that honey-coloured Frontignan. My palate is so used to old Burgundy, it can't deal with them any more. So I say goodbye to Hélène and, beneath the trickle of light rain that falls from the bare trees, I walk into the village.

It is silent, empty and melancholy; night falls quickly. I cross the Place du Monument aux Morts, where the image of a soldier stands guard, painted in the brightest pink and blue. Further along there is an avenue lined with lime trees, then ancient darkish ramparts where an arched doorway opens on to empty space and lets through a chill north wind, and finally the small square in front of the church. At dusk, you can just make out the round loaves of golden bread in the bakery window, lit up by a lamp with a paper shade. In the grey drizzle and fog, the signs hanging in front of the notary and shoemaker seem to float in the air: the shoemaker has a large clog carved out of light wood the size and shape of a cradle. Over the road is the Hôtel des Voyageurs. I push open the door, making a little bell ring, and find myself in the dark, smoky café. A wood-burning stove glows like a red eye; mirrors reflect the marble tabletops, the billiard table, the torn leather settee and the calendar from 1919 with its picture of an Alsatian woman in white stockings standing between two soldiers. Every Sunday, eight farmers (always the same ones) come and play cards in this café. The same words are spoken. You can hear the sound of bottles of red wine being opened and the noise of heavy glasses on the tables. When I come in, voices greet me, one after the other.

"Hello there, Monsieur Sylvestre."

They speak in the slow, gravelly accent that this region has borrowed from neighbouring Burgundy.

I take off my clogs, order some wine and sit down at my usual place, on the left-hand side of the room near the window, from where I can see the hen-house, the laundry and a little garden being drenched by rain.

Everything is permeated by the silence of an autumn evening in a sleepy little village. In front of me is a mirror that frames my wrinkled face, a face so mysteriously changed over the past few years that I scarcely recognise myself. Bah! A sweet, sensual

54

warmth seeps into my bones; I warm my hands at the sputtering wood-burning stove whose smell makes me feel sleepy and slightly sick. The door opens and a young man in a cap appears, or a man in his best Sunday clothes, or a little girl who's come to fetch her father, calling out in a shrill little voice, "You in there? Mum's wantin' you," before she disappears with a burst of laughter.

A few years ago old Declos used to come here every Sunday, like clockwork; he never played cards, he was too mean to risk his money, but he would sit beside the card table, his pipe gripped in the corner of his mouth, and look on silently. Whenever someone asked his advice, he would gesture to them to leave him alone, as if he were refusing to take alms. He's dead and buried now, and in his place is Marc Ohnet, bare-headed and dressed in a leather waistcoat, sitting at a table with a bottle of Beaujolais.

The way a man drinks in company tells you nothing about him, but the way he drinks when alone reveals, without him realising it, the very depths of his soul. There is a particular manner in which a man turns the stem of the glass in his hand, tilts the bottle and watches the wine pour, brings the glass to his lips, then winces and puts it down again when someone calls out to him, picks it up again with a false little cough and downs it in one go, eyes closed, as if seeking forgetfulness at the bottom of the glass — a manner that shows he is preoccupied with something or troubled by worrying thoughts. Marc Ohnet has been spotted; my eight farmers continue to play cards, but now and then they cast furtive glances in his direction. He feigns indifference. It's getting darker. Someone lights the large brass gas lamp hanging from the ceiling; the men put away their cards and begin getting ready to go home. That's when they start talking. First about the weather, the cost of living and the harvest. Then they turn towards Marc Ohnet.

"We haven't seen you in quite a while, Monsieur Marc."

"Not since old Declos's funeral," someone else says.

The young man makes a vague gesture and mutters he's been busy.

They talk about Declos and what he left: "the most beautiful land in the region."

"Now, he knew about farming . . . A miser. A penny was a penny to him. No one round here liked him much, but he knew about farming."

Silence. They've given the dead man their greatest compliment and, in some way, they've made it clear to the young man that they take the side of the dead man and not the living, the old not the young, the husband not the lover. For certain things are known, of course . . . where Brigitte is concerned, at least. They stare at Marc, curiosity burning in their eyes.

"His wife," someone says finally.

Marc looks up and frowns. "What about his wife?"

Cautious little comments slip from the farmers' lips along with the smoke from their pipes:

"His wife . . . She was very young for him, of course, but then, when he married her, he was already rich, and she . . ."

56

"There was Coudray, but it was falling to bits."

"She should have left these parts, of course, it was only thanks to Declos that she kept what she had."

"No one ever knew where she came from."

"She was Mademoiselle Cécile's illegitimate daughter," someone said with a crude laugh.

"I might have thought the same as you if I hadn't known Mademoiselle Cécile. The poor woman wasn't like that, that's for sure. She only ever left the house to go to church."

"Sometimes that's all it takes."

"Maybe, but not Mademoiselle Cécile . . . she didn't have an ounce of wickedness in her. No, the girl she took in was a charity case. Took her as a maid and then got attached to her, adopted her. Madame Declos isn't stupid."

"No, not stupid at all. Just look at how she got her way with the old man . . . Dresses and perfume from Paris, holidays. Anything she wanted. She knows what she's doing. And not only in that way either. You've got to be fair. She knows about farming. Her tenants say you can't fool her. And she's nice to everyone."

"She is. She may be proud of the way she dresses but she's not proud when she talks to you."

"Still, people around here criticise her. She'd do well to be careful."

Suddenly, Ohnet looks up. "Be careful about what?" he asks.

Another silence. The men pull in their chairs, bringing them closer together and at the same time further away from Marc, to demonstrate their disapproval of everything they've guessed is going on, or think they've guessed.

"Careful about her behaviour."

"I think," says Marc, turning his empty glass between his fingers, "I think she couldn't care less about how people see her."

"Be reasonable, Monsieur Marc, be reasonable . . . Her land is hereabouts. She's got to live in these parts. It wouldn't do for people to be pointing their finger at her."

"She could sell her land and leave," one of the farmers says suddenly.

It's old Gonin; his land is right next to Declos's estate. On his patient face appears the harsh, stubborn expression that betrays the men around here when they covet their neighbour's possessions. The others say nothing. I know the game; they've tried it on me. They use it against anyone who isn't from the area, or who's left it, or anyone whom, for some reason or another, they consider undesirable. They didn't like *me* either. I'd abandoned my heritage. I'd preferred other places to where I'd been born. As a result, everything I wished to buy automatically doubled in price; everything I wanted to sell was undervalued. Even in the smallest things I was aware of a malicious intent that was extraordinarily vigilant, always ready to pounce, calculated to make my life unbearable and force me out. I held my ground. I didn't leave. But my land, well, *that* they did get. I see Simon de Saint-Arraud sitting near me, the one who got my meadows, his large dirty hands resting on his knees, and Charles des Roches,

58

who has my farms; while the house where I was born now belongs to the fat farmer with rosy cheeks and a tranquil, sleepy expression who says, with a smile, "Madame Declos would definitely be better off selling. She might know a fair bit about farming, but there's some things a woman can't do."

"She's young; she'll get married again," Marc replies defiantly.

They've all stood up now. One of them opens his big umbrella. Another puts on his clogs and ties a scarf around his neck. When they are at the door, a voice calls out with feigned indifference, "So you think she'll get married again, Monsieur Marc?"

They're all watching him, their eyes wrinkling to hide mocking laughter.

As for Marc, he looks from one to the other, as if he's trying to guess what they're thinking, what they're not saying, as if he's getting ready for a fight. He ends up shrugging his shoulders and saying wearily, with half-closed eyes, "How should I know?"

"But of course you do, Monsieur Marc. Everyone knows you and the old man were pals. Cautious and mistrustful as he was, seems he let you come round any time you wanted, day or night, and sometimes you didn't leave until midnight. You must've seen the widow once or twice since he died, eh?"

"Now and again. Not often."

"How upsetting for you, Monsieur Marc. Two houses where you were well liked and always welcome, then the man of the house dies in both."

"Two houses?"

"Coudray and the Moulin-Neuf."

And, as if satisfied by the way he couldn't help but flinch (so badly that he dropped his glass on to the tiled floor where it shattered), the farmers finally leave. They make a big show of saying goodbye to us: "Goodnight to you, Monsieur Sylvestre. Everything going well for you? That's good. Goodnight to you, Monsieur Marc. Say hello to Madame Declos for us when you see her."

The door opens on an autumn night; you can hear the rain falling, their wooden clogs on the damp ground and, further away, the rustling of a stream. In the grounds of the nearby château, water drips from the branches of enormous trees; the firs weep.

I sit there, smoking my pipe, while Marc Ohnet stares into space. Finally he sighs and calls out, "Bartender! Another bottle of wine."

After Marc Ohnet left this evening, a car full of Parisians arrived and stopped in front of the Hôtel des Voyageurs, just long enough for them to have a drink while a quick repair was made. They came into the café, laughing and talking loudly. A few of the women glanced at me with distaste; the others tried to fix their make-up using the cloudy mirrors that distorted their features, or went over to the windows and looked out at the rain drenching the little cobbled street and the sleepy houses.

"It's so quiet," a young woman said, laughing, then turning away.

Later on their car overtook me on the road. They were going towards Moulins. How many peaceful little places they'll drive through tonight, how many sleepy villages . . . They'll pass silent, sombre country estates and will not begin to imagine the dark, secret life within — a life that they will never come to know. I wonder how Marc Ohnet will sleep tonight, and whether he will dream of the Moulin-Neuf and its green, foaming river.

We thresh the wheat around here. It's the end of summer, time to do the last of the heavy farm work for this season. A day of labour and a day to celebrate. Enormous golden flan cases bake in the oven; since the beginning of the week the children have been shaking plums off the trees so they can decorate them with fruit. There are a huge number of plums this year. The small orchard behind my house is buzzing with bees; the grass is dotted with ripe fruit, the golden skin bursting with little drops of sugar. On threshing day every household takes pride in offering their workers and neighbours the best wine, the thickest cream in the region. To go with them: pies crammed full of cherries and smothered with butter; those small, dry goat cheeses our farmers love so much; bowls of lentils and potatoes; and finally coffee and brandy.

Since my housekeeper had gone to spend the day with her family to help with the meal, I went over to the Erards'. Colette needed to go and visit one of her tenants with François, in a place called Maluret, not far from the Moulin-Neuf. They invited me to come with them. Colette's little boy, who is now two, was to stay at home with his grandmother. Colette found it difficult to leave him. She feels a kind of anxious love for her child that is more a source of torture than joy. Before leaving, she gave Hélène and the maid a thousand instructions, insisting in particular that the child mustn't be allowed to run along the river's edge. Hélène nodded in her usual tender, reasonable way.

"Don't let yourself worry so much, I beg you, Colette. I'm not asking you to forget poor Jean's accident, my darling, I know that's impossible, but don't let it poison your life and your son's life. Think about it. What sort of a man will you make of him if you raise him to be afraid of everything? My poor child, we can't live life for our children, even though we may want to sometimes. Everyone must live and suffer for himself. The greatest favour we can do for our children is to keep our own experiences secret. Believe me, believe your old mother, my darling." She forced herself to laugh to lighten the seriousness of her words.

Colette's eyes, however, were full of tears. "But I wanted to have a life like yours, Mama," she whispered.

Her mother knew what she really meant was: "I wanted to be happy like you."

Hélène sighed. "It was God's will, Colette."

She kissed her daughter, took the baby in her arms and went inside. I watched her walk away, through the garden, proud and beautiful still, despite her greying hair. It is astonishing how she has managed to keep her light, confident bearing all these years. Yes, confident; the confidence of a woman who has never chosen the wrong path, never run, out of breath, to a secret meeting, never stopped, never faltered beneath the weight of a guilty secret . . .

Colette seemed to be thinking the same and put it into words. "Mama is like the evening of a beautiful day . . ." she said, taking her father's arm.

He smiled at her. "Now, now, my darling . . . Your evening will have the same grace and serenity. Come on, hurry up now, we have a long way to go."

The whole way there, Colette seemed more cheerful than she'd been since Jean had died. François was driving. She was sitting next to me, in the back of the car. It was a lovely warm day, with just a hint of autumn in the air. Beneath the blue sky, colder and crisper than in August, only a scattering of crimson leaves and the occasional breeze foretold the end of summer. After a while, Colette began to laugh and talk excitedly, something she hadn't done in a very long time. She recalled the long outings she'd been on with her parents, along this very road, when she was a child.

"Do you remember, Papa? Henri and Loulou hadn't been born yet. Georges was the youngest and he was left at home with the maid, which made me feel so happy and proud. What a treat! Goodness, I'd had to wait for it, though, sometimes as long as a month. Then we'd get the picnic baskets ready. Oh, all those lovely cakes . . . They just don't taste the same any more. Mama kneaded the pastry, her arms covered in flour up to the elbow, remember? Sometimes friends came along, but we often went alone. After lunch, Mama made me lie down on the grass to rest, while you read. That's right, isn't it? You read Verlaine and Rimbaud, and I so wanted to run about . . . But I'd just lie there, half listening, thinking about my toys, about the long afternoon that was drifting away, and savouring the . . . the perfect happiness I felt then."

As she talked, her voice grew deeper and lower, and you could tell she'd forgotten her father and was talking to herself; she fell silent for a moment, then continued, "Do you remember, Papa, the time the car broke down? We had to get out and walk, and because I was so tired, you and Mama asked a farmer who was passing by with his cart full of lopped branches if I could ride with him. I remember he made a kind of roof out of the foliage to shelter me from the sun; you walked behind the cart and the farmer led his horse. Then, because you thought no one could see you, you stopped and kissed . . . Do you remember? I suddenly popped my head out from underneath the branches of my little house and shouted, 'I can see you!' And you both started to laugh. Do you remember? And it was that evening we stopped at a big house where there was very little furniture, no electricity and a great brass candelabrum in the middle of the table . . . Oh, it's so funny, I'd forgotten about that, and now it's coming back to me. Maybe it was just a dream."

"No it wasn't," said François. "That was Coudray, your old Aunt Cécile's house. You were thirsty and crying, so we stopped to ask for some milk for you; your mother didn't want to, I can't recall why, but you were screaming so much that in the end there was no other way of keeping you quiet. You were six then."

"Wait a minute . . . I remember it all very well now. There was a spinster with a yellow shawl around her shoulders and a young girl of about fifteen. The girl must have been her ward."

"Yes, that was your friend, Brigitte Declos, or should I say Brigitte Ohnet, since she's about to marry that young man."

Colette fell silent and stared pensively out of the window. "Are they definitely getting married, then?" she asked finally.

"Yes, I've heard their banns are being published on Sunday."

"Oh."

Her lips were trembling but she spoke quite calmly. "I hope they'll be happy."

She didn't say another word until François was about to take the long way round to Maluret, to avoid passing the Moulin-Neuf. She hesitated for a moment, then touched his shoulder. "Papa, please don't think it will be painful for me to see the mill again. Quite the opposite. You see, I left the day poor Jean was buried, and everything was so solemn and sad that it left me with a very disturbing memory of the place . . . and . . . it's not fair, somehow . . . Not fair for Jean. I can't explain it, but . . . He did everything he could to make me happy, to make me love the house. I'd like to exorcise the memory," she added, her voice low and strained. "I'd like to see the river again. Maybe it would cure me of my fear of water."

"That fear will disappear by itself, Colette. What good would it do to . . . ?"

"Do you think so? Because I often dream about the river and it seems sinister to me. To see it again, in the sunlight, would do me good I think. Please, Papa."

"If that's what you want," François said as he turned the car back.

We passed Coudray (Colette looked sad and jealous as she glanced towards its open windows), then we took the road through the woods and crossed the bridge. I saw the mill up ahead. Some farmers noticed us go by, but since they didn't acknowledge us I asked Colette if they were the tenants I'd met, the ones who'd sent their farmhand to Coudray the night of the accident.

"No," she said. "That was the family of Jean's nanny. After my husband's death, she was unhappy here. Their lease expired in October and they didn't want to renew it. They've gone to Sainte-Arnould."

As she spoke, she touched her father's shoulder to get him to stop. As I've said, it was a lovely day, but so nearly autumn that, as soon as you were out of the sun, it felt cold and everything looked suddenly dismal. That never happens at the height of summer, when even the shade gives off a secret warmth. As we were looking at the Moulin-Neuf, a cloud hid the sun; the light that played on the river disappeared. Colette sank back and closed her eyes. François restarted the engine. After driving for a few moments he whispered, "I shouldn't have listened to you."

"No," Colette replied softly, "I don't think I'll ever be able to forget . . ."

At Maluret they were finishing their meal, their "four o'clock", as they call it here, before going back to work.

Everyone was in the main room. Maluret is a château that used to belong to the de Coudray barons. Aunt Cécile's Coudray was also part of the estate a hundred and fifty years ago. That was when the bankrupt baron's family left the region and their land was split up. Jean Dorin's grandfather built the Moulin-Neuf and bought the château, but he hadn't worked out the costs properly, or perhaps, blinded by his desire to own it, hadn't seen what a sorry state the house was in. He soon realised that he wasn't rich enough to restore it and turned it into a tenanted farm, which it has remained to this day. It looks both proud and pitiful, with its great courtyard, now home to the hen-houses and rabbit hutches, its terrace, cleared of chestnut trees and hung with washing, and its high gate topped by the crumbling family coat of arms, shattered during the Revolution. The people who live here (their name is Dupont, but they're called the Malurets: it's a custom in these parts to confuse the person with his land to such an extent that they become one and the same), these people are far from friendly. They have a suspicious, almost primitive nature. Maluret is surrounded by extensive woods (the former seigneurial park, which has run wild) and is far from the village. In winter the farmers can go six or eight months without seeing a soul. Not that they have anything in common with our rich, slick-talking landowners whose daughters wear silk stockings and put on make-up on Sundays. The Malurets have no money and are even stingier than they are poor. Their sullen nature is a perfect match for the rickety old château with its bare rooms.

The floorboards creak beneath your feet; stones fall from the great wall and bluish slate tiles from the roof. The pigs are kept in the former library; woollen fleeces cure inside the house. The fireplaces are so enormous that fires are never lit: they would devour the entire forest. There is one exquisite little room with a painted alcove and a window at the back; the alcove contains their stock of potatoes for the winter and around the window are strung golden garlands of onions.

François says it's particularly difficult to do business with the Malurets. I can't now remember exactly why he'd come to see the head of the household; in any case, they both went out to look at the roof of a barn that had caught fire. The rest of the Malurets, along with the servants, friends and neighbours who'd come to help with the threshing, continued slowly to eat their meal. The men kept their hats on, as was the custom. Colette went to sit in the arch of the large sculpted fireplace and I sat down at the big table. I knew a few of the people there, but many were unfamiliar, or perhaps they simply seemed so and, in fact, they had just grown old, like me — so old they looked like strangers. Among them were the farmers who had once been tenants of the Moulin-Neuf, the ones who left after Jean died. I asked after their old mother, Jean's nanny: she had died. There were ten or twelve children, something like that; among them was the young lad who'd come to tell Brigitte about the accident. He was sixteen or seventeen and for the first time, no doubt, he was drinking like a man. He seemed tipsy; his eyes were red and swollen, and his cheeks burned scarlet. He was watching Colette with a strange intensity. Suddenly he called out to her from the end of the table, "So, that's it, then, you don't live up there no more?"

"No," said Colette, "I've gone back to live with my parents."

He opened his mouth as if to say something else, but François came in, so he kept quiet. He poured himself another large glass of wine.

"You'll have a drink with us, won't you?" asked Monsieur Maluret, gesturing to his wife to get out a few more bottles.

François accepted.

"And you, Madame?" he asked Colette.

Colette got up and came over to join us, for you can't insult your hosts by refusing to have a drink, especially during these big country get-togethers. The men were all mildly intoxicated in the heavy, morose way of farmworkers. Up before dawn, they could feel ten hours of work in their muscles and had wolfed down their food with giant appetites. The women busied themselves around the stove. They started teasing the young lad, who was sitting beside me. He replied with a kind of rude impudence that made everyone laugh. You could tell he was drunk in a bad way, looking for a fight — that state of intoxication where you can't hold your tongue, as we say around here. The heat in the room, the smoke from the pipes, the smell of the tarts on the table, the buzzing of the wasps around the overflowing jam pots, the loud, resonant laughter of the farmers, all this must have contributed to the dreamlike state you float in when

70

you can't hold your drink. And he never stopped staring at Colette.

"Don't you miss the Moulin-Neuf?" François asked him absent-mindedly.

"Hell, no, we're better off up here."

"Well, that's gratitude for you," said Colette, smiling uncomfortably. "Don't you remember the lovely jam sandwiches I used to make you?"

"'Course I remember."

"Well, that's good."

"'Course I remember," the lad said again.

He was turning his fork over and over in his heavy hand and continuing to stare at Colette in the most intense way.

"I remember everything," he said suddenly. "Many people might've forgot, but not me, I remember everything."

By chance, just as he spoke, all the other conversation stopped and his words resounded around the room so loudly that everyone was shocked. Colette went very white and quiet. Surprised, her father asked, "What do you mean, my boy?"

"I mean, what I mean is that if anyone here has forgotten how Monsieur Jean died, well, not me, I remember."

"No one's forgotten," I said, and I gestured for Colette to get up and move away from the table; but she stayed put.

François saw something was up, but since he was miles away from imagining the truth, instead of making the kid shut up he leaned towards him and questioned him anxiously. "Do you mean you saw something that night? Tell me, please. This is very serious."

"Pay no attention," said Maluret. "You can see he's drunk."

Good Lord, I thought, they know, they all know. But if this imbecile doesn't talk, none of them will ever breathe a word. The farmers around here don't gossip and would rather walk through fire than get involved in other people's business.

But they knew; they all looked away, embarrassed.

"Come on. Behave yourself," said Maluret brusquely. "You've had enough to drink. Back to work."

But François was upset and grabbed the boy by the sleeve. "Don't go. You know something we don't, I'm sure of it. I've often thought his death was odd; you don't fall from a bridge accidentally when you've been crossing it every day since you were a child and you know every step of the way. And Monsieur Jean had brought back a lot of money from Nevers that day. His wallet was never found. We all thought it had got lost when he fell and was carried away by the river. But maybe it was simply that he was robbed, robbed and murdered. So listen, if you saw something we don't know about, it's your duty to tell us. Isn't it, Colette?" he added, turning towards his daughter.

She didn't have the strength to reply, so she simply nodded.

"My poor darling, this must be very painful for you. Go outside, let me talk to this boy alone."

She shook her head. Everyone was silent. The lad seemed to sober up all of a sudden. You could see him

72

trembling as he answered François's pressing questions. "All right, then, I saw someone shove him into the river. I told my grandma the same night, but she said I wasn't allowed to tell anyone."

"But look here, if a crime's been committed you have to go to the police, punish the culprit.

"These people are unbelievable," François whispered to me. "They can watch a man being murdered before their very eyes and still not say a word 'to avoid getting involved'. They saw what happened to our poor Jean and for two years they've kept quiet. Colette, tell him he doesn't have the right to keep silent! Do you hear me, boy, Monsieur Jean's widow is ordering you to speak up."

"That true, Madame?" he asked, looking up at her.

"Yes." She sighed and buried her face in her hands.

The women had abandoned the washing up and come out of the kitchen. They stood and listened, their hands clasped over their stomachs.

"Well," said the lad, "first off, you should know that my dad had punished me that night, because of a cow I didn't clean up like I should've. He hit me and threw me out without supper. I was so mad, I didn't feel like going back in. They kept calling me when it was bedtime, but I pretended not to hear. Dad said, 'Fine, if he wants to be that way, let him sleep outdoors, that'll teach him.' I really wanted to go in then, but I didn't want anyone making fun of me. So I sneaked into the kitchen and got some bread and cheese. Then I went to hide down by the river. You know the place, Madame, that spot under the willows where you sometimes used to go and read in summer. That's where I was when I heard Monsieur Jean's car. 'Strange,' I said to myself, 'he's home sooner than expected.' He wasn't due back till the next day, remember? But he stopped the car in the meadow and stood next to it for a really long time — so long that I got scared, I don't know why. It was a funny kind of night. The wind was whistling, all the trees were shaking ... I think he must have been by the car because I couldn't see him. To get back to the mill, he would've had to cross the bridge, and pass right in front of me. I thought maybe he was hiding, or waiting for someone. It lasted such a long time I fell asleep. A noise on the bridge woke me up. Two men fighting. It all happened so quick I didn't have a chance to leg it. One of the men threw the other one in the water and took off. I heard Monsieur Jean cry out as he fell; I recognised his voice. He shouted, 'Oh, God!' Then there was nothing but the sound of the river. So I ran straight home and woke everyone up to tell them what'd happened. Grandma said, 'Now listen you, all you have to do is keep quiet, you didn't see nothing, didn't hear nothing, understand?' I hadn't been home five minutes when you got there, Madame, calling for help, saying your husband had been drowned and asking us to look for the body. So Dad went down to the mill. Grandma'd been Monsieur Jean's nanny. 'I'll go and find a sheet and wrap him in it with my own hands,' she said, 'that poor boy' and Mum sent me to

74

Coudray to tell them the master was dead. That's it. That's all I know."

"Are you sure you weren't dreaming? You'd repeat what you told us to a judge?"

He hesitated slightly, then replied, "Yes, I would. It's the truth."

"And the man who pushed Monsieur Jean into the water, do you know who he was?"

There was a very long silence as everyone stared at the boy. Only Colette looked away. She had her hands clasped in front of her now; the tips of her fingers were trembling.

"No idea," the boy said at last.

"You didn't catch a glimpse of him? Not even for a second? It was a clear night, after all."

"I was still half asleep. I saw two men fighting. That's all."

"And Monsieur Jean didn't cry out for help?"

"If he did, I didn't hear him."

"Which way did the other man go?"

"Into the woods."

François rubbed his eyes. "This is incredible. It's . . . it's unbelievable. Yes, an accident on the bridge is possible, but only if Jean had been feeling ill or faint: you don't slip on a bridge you've crossed ten times a day for twenty-five years. Colette said that 'he must have blacked out'. But why? He didn't suffer from vertigo; he was fit and healthy. On the other hand we all know there were robberies committed in the area that year, and fires set, and that several prowlers were arrested. I did sometimes wonder whether this accident

75

wasn't an accident at all, whether poor Jean was murdered. But still, this lad's story is very strange indeed. Why didn't Jean go straight home? You're quite sure he stayed beside the car for a long time?"

"You were sleeping," I said to the lad. "You said so yourself. When you're asleep, you can lose all sense of time, you know. Sometimes you think only a few minutes have passed when, half the night has gone. And then, sometimes, you can have a long dream and think you've been asleep for hours when you've only closed your eyes for a second."

"That's very true," several people said.

"Here's what I think happened," I said, "The boy was sleeping; he woke up; he heard the sound of the car; he went back to sleep. It felt as if a long time had passed when, in fact, there were no more than a few seconds between the moment Jean arrived and when he crossed the bridge. A prowler — maybe someone who knew there weren't many people at home that night since even the servant had gone — this prowler got into the mill. Jean caught him by surprise. He heard footsteps, ran outside. Jean tried to stop him. The man fought him off and, during the struggle, he pushed Jean into the water. That's what must have happened."

"We have to report it to the police," said François. "This is a serious matter."

They noticed that Colette was crying. The men gradually got to their feet.

"Come on, everyone out," said Maluret. "Let's get back to work."

They finished their drinks and left. Only the women remained, going about their business in the large kitchen without looking at Colette. Her father took her arm, helped her into the car and we left.

It was a warm evening, so I sat down on the bench outside the kitchen, from where I can see my little garden. For a long time I only wanted it to provide me with vegetables for my soup, but for several years now I've been taking better care of it. I planted the rose bushes myself, saved the vine that was dying, dug, weeded, pruned the fruit trees. Little by little, I have become attached to this tiny piece of land. On summer evenings, at dusk, the sound of ripe fruit coming away from the trees and falling gently on to the grass fills me with a sense of happiness. Night descends . . . but you can't really call it night: the azure blue of the day grows misty, turns almost green; colour slowly melts away, leaving a delicate hue that is midway between translucent pearl and steel grey. But every shape is perfectly clear: the well, the cherry trees, the little low wall, the forest and the head of the cat who's playing at my feet, nipping at my shoe. It's then that the housekeeper goes home; she puts on the light in the kitchen and everything around me is suddenly lost in darkness. Dusk is the best time of day and, of course, the time Colette chose to come and ask for my advice. I was quite cold towards her, so cold, in fact, that she seemed disconcerted. But it's like this: when I go out and mix with other people voluntarily, I agree, more or less, to get involved in their odd lives; but when I've climbed back into my hole, I want to be left in peace, so don't come bothering me with your loves and your regrets.

"What can *I* do to help you?" I said to Colette, who was crying. "Nothing. I can't see what you're so tormented about. It's your parents' decision whether or not to follow up that little idiot's story. Go and talk to them. They're not children. They know about life. Tell them you had a lover and that he killed your husband . . . What exactly did happen?"

"I was waiting for Marc that night. Jean wasn't supposed to get home until the next day. I still don't know what happened or why he came back early."

"You don't know why, you innocent thing? Because someone told him that you'd be meeting your lover that night, that's why."

She shuddered and lowered her head every time I said the word "lover". I could hear her sighing in the darkness. She was ashamed. But what other word could I use?

"I think it must have been the servant who told him," she said at last. "Anyway, I was expecting Marc at midnight. My husband, who'd been watching out, saw him cross the bridge and threw himself at him. But Marc was stronger." (What unintentional pride rang in her voice!) "Marc didn't want to hurt him! He was just defending himself . . . But then he flew into a rage. He

**79**

picked Jean up, dragged him to the spot where there's no handrail and hurled him into the water."

"It wasn't the first time Marc had come to your house, was it?"

"No . . ."

"You weren't faithful to poor Jean for very long, were you?"

No reply.

"Yet no one forced you to marry him, did they?"

"No. I loved him. But Marc . . . The first time I saw him, the very first time, he could have done whatever he liked with me, do you understand? Does that seem unbelievable to you?"

"Not at all; I've known it happen before."

"You're making fun of me. But at least understand that it wasn't in my nature to be a bad wife. If I were the kind of person who simply had affairs, I'm sure everything would seem very simple: I had an adulterous affair that ended badly, nothing more. But that's just the problem. I was supposed to have the kind of life that Mama had. I was supposed to be pure-hearted, to grow old gracefully like her, with no regrets. Then suddenly . . . I remember I'd spent the day with Jean. We were so happy. I went over to Brigitte Declos's house. We were close. She was young. I didn't have any friends my own age. And — it's odd — we even look alike. I told her that several times; she laughed, but she obviously thought I was right because she used to reply, 'We could be sisters.' It was at her house that I met Marc for the first time. And I knew at once that she was his mistress, that she was in love with him and I felt . . .

strangely jealous. Yes, I was jealous even before I fell in love. But jealous isn't quite the right word. No, I was envious. I desperately envied the kind of happiness that Jean couldn't give me. Not a physical happiness, you understand, but a burning in my soul, something that was beyond what I'd been calling love. I went back home. I cried all night. I hated myself. If Marc had left me alone I would have forgotten all about it, but he liked me and wouldn't stop pursuing me. So, one day, a few weeks later . . ."

"I see."

"I knew it couldn't last. I understood he'd end up marrying Brigitte once her elderly husband died. I thought . . . no, actually, I didn't think at all. I loved him. I told myself that as long as Jean didn't know anything, it was as if there wasn't anything to know. Sometimes I had nightmares: I dreamt that he would find out, but only later on, much later on, when we were old. And I felt he'd forgive me. How could I have foreseen this terrible tragedy? I killed him. I killed my husband. It's because of me that he's dead. I keep saying it to myself over and over again and I feel as if I'm going mad."

"Your tears won't bring him back. Now, calm down and think about how you can avoid a scandal, since, naturally, any serious inquiry will easily reveal the truth. Everyone around here knows what really happened."

"But how can I avoid a scandal? How?"

"Your father mustn't go to the police and, to make sure he doesn't, he'll have to know . . ."

"I can't! I won't tell him anything. I can't. I wouldn't dare . . ."

"But you're mad. Anyone would think you were afraid of your parents; your parents love you."

"But how can you not understand? You know the life they have together, their wonderful relationship, the high ideal they have of married love. How do you think I, their daughter, could admit that I was unfaithful to my husband in a contemptible way, that I had another man in my house when my husband was away and that my lover killed him? Isn't it enough that I have one tragedy on my conscience?" she cried, bursting into tears.

Once she'd calmed down a bit, I again asked her what she wanted me to do.

"Couldn't you tell them . . .?"

"What difference would that make?"

"Oh, I don't know. But I think I'd die if I had to tell them myself. You . . . You could make them understand that it was a moment of madness, that I'm not completely evil and depraved, that I myself don't even understand how I could have acted the way I did. Would you, dear Cousin Silvio?"

I thought about it and replied, "No."

Poor Colette let out a cry of surprise and despair. "No? Why not?"

"For several reasons. First of all — and I can't explain why, so you'll just have to take my word for it — if this bad news came from me, as you'd like, your mother would suffer even more. Don't ask me why. I can't tell you. And second, because I don't want to get involved in your problems. I don't want to be running back and forth from one member of the family to the next calming everyone down, reporting what was said, giving advice and spouting moral philosophy. I'm old, Colette, and all I want is a quiet life. At my age, one feels a kind of coldness ... Of course, you can't understand that, any more than I can understand your love affairs and foolish mistakes. However hard I try, I can't see things the way you do. To you, Jean's death is an horrific catastrophe. To me ... well, I've seen so many die. He was a poor, jealous, clumsy lad who's better off where he is. You blame yourself for his death? The way I see it, the only things to blame are chance or destiny. Your affair with Marc? Well, you got some pleasure from it. What else do you want? And the same goes for your parents; I wouldn't be able to stop myself telling them truths that would surprise and upset them, good souls that they are ..."

"Cousin Silvio," she interrupted, "I sometimes think ..." She hesitated, then continued, "You don't admire them the way I do."

"No one deserves to be admired so passionately. Just as no one deserves to be despised with too much indignation ..."

"Or loved with too much tenderness ..."

"Perhaps ... I don't know. Love, you know ... At my age the blood no longer burns, you feel cold," I said again.

Suddenly, Colette took my hand. The poor child, how warm she was! "I feel sorry for you," she said softly.

"And I feel sorry for you," I said rather harshly. "You torture yourself over so many things."

We sat very still for a long time. The night was beginning to feel damp. The frogs were croaking.

"What will you do after I leave?" she asked.

"What I do every night."

"What's that?"

"Well, I'll shut the gate. I'll lock the doors. I'll wind the clock. I'll get my cards and play a few games of Solitaire. I'll have a glass of wine. I won't think about anything. I'll go to bed. I won't sleep much. Instead I'll dream with my eyes open. I'll see people and things from the past. As for you, well, you'll go home, you'll feel miserable, you'll cry, you'll get out Jean's photograph and ask his forgiveness, you'll regret the past, fear the future. I can't say which of us will have a better night."

She said nothing for a moment.

"I'll be going now," she whispered with a sigh.

I walked her to the gate. She got on her bicycle and left.

Later, Colette told me that she hadn't gone home, but had continued on to Coudray. She was so frantic that she felt she must do something, at all costs, to try to overcome her grief. She told me that while I'd been talking to her she'd realised that, after herself, or even before herself, the person who would benefit most from avoiding a scandal was Brigitte Declos, Marc's fiancée. She was determined to see her, to tell her what had happened and ask her advice. Did Brigitte know the details of how Jean had died? She must have guessed most of it . . . Anyway, it had happened over two years ago; Marc and Colette weren't seeing each other any more. She couldn't be jealous of something that had happened in the past. Her only thought would be to save the man she was going to marry in two weeks' time . . . Perhaps Colette wasn't overly concerned by the idea that she might cast a slight shadow over their happiness. In any case, it was in the interests of all three of them. So she went to see Brigitte, who had dined with her fiancé's family and was now at home alone.

She told Brigitte that Marc was in great danger.

Brigitte understood immediately. She went very white and asked what Colette was talking about.

"Do you know that it was Marc who killed my husband?" Colette asked harshly.

"Yes," she replied.

"He admitted it to you, then?"

"He didn't need to tell me. I guessed what had happened the same night."

"When she said that," Colette told me, "I suddenly thought to myself, 'She was the one who told Jean. She knew that Marc was cheating on her with me. She thought: *Her husband will break them up*. She knew Jean was shy and not very strong. She never would have imagined he'd attack Marc the way he did. She thought we'd talk things through, that I'd be afraid of a scandal, that I'd worry about hurting my parents, all of which would lead me to give up Marc for good. That's all she wanted. Jean's death was something terrible and unexpected for her as well.'"

At first, Brigitte tried to avoid answering Colette's questions, but finally she confessed that she'd written to Jean the day before he died, "spelling it out for him, I admit it", telling him that Colette would be waiting for Marc Ohnet to spend the night with her.

"If I could have imagined . . . Both of us have been punished terribly. Don't be envious of me. I may have kept the man I love, but think how much we've suffered. Think of the danger he's in. Our courts aren't lenient on crimes of passion. He could say it was in self-defence, but who knows if they'd believe him? Perhaps they'd think he ambushed your husband to get rid of him . . . And even if he were acquitted, what would our life be like here, where everyone hates me and no one likes him much either? Yet everything we have is here."

"You're not married yet," Colette had said. "You could call it off."

"No," replied Brigitte, "I love him and this tragedy was mostly my fault. I won't abandon the man I love because he's in trouble. You must convince your father not to go to the police. If nothing is official, no one will say anything. We'll have to be brave and stand up to all the rumours, all the prying. I'm sure we can do it."

They talked through the night, "almost as friends", according to Colette. Both of them loved Marc and wanted to save him. Colette was also terrified for her parents and her son.

"You're right," she said eventually, "my mother and father must know the truth. But it will be horrible for me. I can't tell them. They won't understand. They'll be devastated. Once I'm standing face to face with them, looking at their dear old honest faces, I'll be so ashamed that I won't be able to say a word."

Brigitte had been silent for a long time. Finally, she looked at the time and said, "It's very late. Go home now. Tomorrow morning make up some excuse to leave. Stay away for a few days. *I'll* go and see your parents and tell them what happened. It may be easier than you think."

"I believed my parents would prefer to hear the truth from someone else," Colette told me. "There's such a sense of propriety between parents and children . . . When I was little it embarrassed me to see my mother naked. And I remember being worried they might guess thoughts I considered shameful, but which I didn't hesitate to confide in any one of my friends or our old maid. My parents were different, they were above human weakness and I still think of them that way. I thought, 'They'll find out everything, but I'll stay away for several days. They'll have time to compose themselves. By the time I get home, they'll understand that they must never talk to me about any of it, never. They'll keep quiet. They know how to keep quiet. And then it will be as if this hideous thing had never happened.'"

The next morning François and Hélène came to see me. Hélène was terribly upset. Even though she had no idea of the truth, she was loath to go to the police, saying it would only cause her daughter more suffering.

But François, a true bourgeois who respected the law, believed it was his duty: "It was some prowler, some deranged drunk who must have done it. Perhaps one of the Poles who work on the farms. Whoever the culprit might be, don't forget that someone who's got away with a crime once might be tempted to rob or murder again. We would be responsible, indirectly. If innocent blood were shed again, it would be partly our fault."

"What does Colette say about it?" I asked.

"Colette? Would you believe it, she's gone away," Hélène replied. "She got a lift to the station this morning and took the eight o'clock train to Nevers. She left me a note saying she didn't want to wake me but, last night, she broke the little Empire mirror that belonged to Jean and she wants to have it repaired straight away. She wrote that she'll take advantage of her trip to go and see one of her old school friends in Nevers and be back in two or three days. Naturally, we'll wait until she's home before deciding what to do. Poor darling! All this business about a broken mirror is just an excuse. The truth is, she was very upset by what that boy said and wants to get away from this place that brings back so many sad memories, maybe so she wouldn't have to hear people saying Jean's name. She was like that when she was little. When her grandmother died, Colette got up and left the room every time someone mentioned the poor woman. One day, I asked her why and she said, 'I can't help crying and I don't want everyone to see me cry.'"

She's stalling, I thought to myself. Maybe she'll write to them from Nevers to tell them the truth, to avoid the face-to-face confession she's dreading so much.

I also thought she might have gone to see a priest. Later on I found out she'd been seeing one for some time and that he'd advised her to tell her family what had happened, adding that it was appropriate penance for her sin. But her fear of causing her beloved parents suffering had forced her to remain silent. Actually, I imagined all sorts of reasons why Colette might have gone away, but of course I never guessed that she had involved Brigitte Declos.

"I think Hélène is right," I said to François. "It will be very painful for Colette to have the police prying into her private life with her husband."

"Good Lord, those poor children had nothing to hide."

"As for the killer (if there really was a killer, if that lad wasn't lying), he surely would have left the area a long time ago."

But François just shook his head. "That doesn't mean he won't commit another crime when he's drunk or out of money. If he kills someone in another place, how will it make me less responsible? It will be on my conscience whether it's in the Saône-et-Loire, the Lot-et-Garonne, the North or the Midi." He looked at his wife. "I don't really understand what there is to discuss. You surprise me, Hélène. You have such a sense of right and wrong, how can you of all people not feel how degrading it would be to cover up a crime simply because it might upset us?"

"Not us, François, our daughter."

"Doing our duty has nothing to do with our love for our child," François replied softly. "But what's the point of going on about it? When Colette gets back, we'll talk it through, and I'm sure she'll come round to my way of thinking."

It was late morning and they needed to get home. They'd walked to Mont-Tharaud and asked if I wanted to walk back with them. The whole way we avoided the subject of children by tacit agreement, but it was obvious that all they could think about was the tragedy and the dramatic events of the previous day.

Hélène invited me to stay for lunch. I accepted. We'd just finished eating when someone rang the bell. The maid came in and said it was Madame Brigitte Declos.

Hélène went very pale. As for François, he seemed surprised, but he told the maid to bring her into the little study where we had come to drink our coffee; we stood up to greet her.

The study is a charming little room, full of books, with two large armchairs next to the fireplace. For more than twenty years my cousins have spent their peaceful evenings in this room, he sitting in one of the armchairs reading a book, she in the other, doing some embroidery, the clock between them, always ticking, slowly, calmly — the very picture of conjugal happiness.

Brigitte came in and looked around with curiosity: she'd never seen this room, having visited my cousins' house just once, the day of Colette's wedding. Then, she'd only gone as far as the sitting room, which is gloomy and formal. Here, everything was a testament to happiness and deep mutual love. People may not tell the truth, but flowers, books, portraits, lamps — the gentle, aged look of such things — reveal more than people's faces. There was a time when I often looked carefully at all these objects and thought, "They made each other happy. It's as if the past didn't exist. They're happy and they love each other." Later on it was so obvious that I stopped thinking about it and, besides, it didn't matter to me any more.

Brigitte looked pale and thin; she was less . . . wild and sensual, if I can put it that way, more like a mature woman. What I mean is she'd lost that arrogant confidence that comes with happiness; she seemed worried and there was something else in her expression as she glanced around her, a kind of defiance, resentment and, at the same time, curiosity and anguish. She refused the cup of coffee that Hélène automatically offered her.

"I have come to beg you, Monsieur Erard," she said, her voice quiet and shaking a little, "not to do what you plan, not to go to the police about your son-in-law's death. This is very serious. If the truth came out, it would cause even more problems."

"More problems? For whom?"

"For you."

"Do you know who killed Jean?"

"Yes. It was Marc Ohnet. My fiancé."

François stood up and began to pace nervously about the room. Hélène didn't utter a word. Brigitte waited for a moment, then, seeing that no one was saying anything, continued, "We're going to be married in a few days. We love each other. It would cause a terrible scandal that would destroy our lives and wouldn't bring back your poor son-in-law."

"But, Madame," exclaimed François, "do you realise what you're saying? ... Whether the murderer is a tramp, some vagabond or Marc Ohnet, your fiancé, doesn't change the fact that a crime has been committed and that the man responsible must be punished. Are you actually saying that you're begging me to do this for the sake of your happiness, you who've destroyed my daughter's happiness? These two men were fighting over you, I suppose? Were they both courting you, perhaps?"

François is a good man but he does have one fault: he keeps to himself for the most part and when he's very upset he expresses himself "like a book", as they say around here. I don't know why, but I'd never been struck by it as much as today. I couldn't help smiling

93

and Brigitte smiled too: there was not much kindness in her smile.

"Monsieur Erard, I swear to you that those two men never fought over me and that Jean Dorin never courted me. You do him an injustice. He was faithful to his wife; and as for me, I wouldn't have given him a second look. I've been Marc Ohnet's mistress for four years. I love him and have never loved anyone else."

She looked at him with an air of bravado that infuriated François.

"Aren't you ashamed of yourself?"

"Ashamed? Why?"

"Because you've done something wrong," he replied coldly. "Your husband may have been old, but it was your duty to respect him. It is revolting to have been unfaithful to a man who took you in when you had nothing, who spoiled you and loved you, and who left you his fortune. You took his money and bought yourself a young lover . . ."

"This has nothing to do with money."

"It always has to do with money, Madame. I'm an old man and you're a child. Of course, what you do is none of my business, but since you think it appropriate to confide in me, perhaps you will allow me to explain this hideous thing you can't see. You cheated on your husband in a vile manner. He leaves you a fortune. You and your fiancé will live off that fortune. A fine pair! And you'll have the memory of a crime . . . since you're telling me that your miserable lover killed our poor Jean. What a wonderful future you'll have together, Madame. You're young now. All you can see is what

94

gives you pleasure. Think of what it will be like for the two of you when you're old."

"We'll be as happy as you are," she said quietly.

"No, you won't."

"Are you sure of that?"

Her voice sounded so strange that Hélène made a movement towards her and let out a sort of plaintive cry.

Brigitte seemed to hesitate, then continued, "Your morals are beyond reproach," she said. "Yet, wasn't Madame Erard a widow when you married her?"

"What are you getting at? How dare you compare yourself with my wife?"

"I mean no offence," she replied in the same quiet, steady tone, "I'm just asking . . . Madame Erard was married before, like me, to an old, sick husband. She was faithful to him, but I'd like her to tell me whether it was always easy or pleasant to remain faithful."

"I didn't love my first husband, it's true," said Hélène, "but I didn't marry him against my will. So I had no right to complain and neither do you . . ."

"There are many things that influence our will," Brigitte said bitterly, "poverty, for example, or being abandoned . . ."

"Being abandoned, oh . . ."

"Yes, exactly. Do you think I wasn't abandoned?"

"But Mademoiselle Cécile . . ."

"Mademoiselle Cécile did everything she could for me: she took the place of my mother. Still, my mother never gave me a second thought. When I was left all alone she made no attempt to contact me. So the first man who came along . . . Do you really think that a young woman of twenty willingly marries an old farmer of sixty? A harsh, stingy old man? Willingly? You call that willingly? And your own daughter, your *legitimate* daughter" (she emphasised the word) "Colette really did marry Jean Dorin willingly, but that didn't stop her becoming Marc Ohnet's mistress. Ask her about it; she'll tell you how she allowed Marc to visit her at night, how her husband found out and how he died."

Then she told us what had happened. François and Hélène listened in stunned silence. Tears were streaming down Hélène's face.

"Are you crying because of your daughter?" Brigitte asked. "No need to worry. She'll forget, things like this always get forgotten. It's easy to live with the memory of a bad deed, as you put it, or even a crime. You've had a good life," she added, turning towards Hélène.

"A crime . . ." the poor woman protested softly.

"I call it a crime to have a child and abandon it. At any rate that's worse than cheating on an old husband you don't love. What do you think, Monsieur Erard?"

"What do you mean?"

Hélène was trembling but managed to compose herself. She gestured to Brigitte to be silent. Then she turned towards her husband. "Since you must know, I prefer you hear it from me. This child has the right to speak as she does: I had a lover before we were married" (her wrinkled face blushed) "an affair that lasted only a few weeks. I had a baby girl. I didn't want to tell you what had happened or force the child on you. But I didn't want to abandon her either. My half-sister, Cécile, was free and alone; she took care of Brigitte. I thought she was happy. Little by little . . ."

She fell silent.

"Little by little, you forgot all about me," said Brigitte. "But *I've* always known . . . One day you came to Coudray with your husband and Colette, who was still very young. She was crying; she wanted a drink. You sat her on your lap; you kissed her. She had such a pretty little dress and a gold necklace . . . And I . . . I was so jealous. You didn't even look at me . . ."

"I didn't dare. I was so afraid I'd give myself away . . ."

"That's not true," said Brigitte. "You had simply forgotten all about me. But I always knew . . . Cécile told me. She hated you, your sister Cécile. She hated you almost without realising it. You were younger, prettier, happier than she was. You have been happy. You know that's true. Well, let me live as you have done. Don't be too harsh towards Colette, who thinks you're a saint, who'd rather die than let you see her for who she really is. As for me, well, I'm not as particular. You won't go to the police, will you, Monsieur Erard? These are family matters and must be kept to ourselves."

She waited for a reply, but none came. She got up, carefully picked up her handbag and gloves, walked over to the mirror and adjusted her hat. Just then the maid came in to take away the coffee cups, full of attentiveness and curiosity. Hélène accompanied the young woman through the garden to the gate.

"Since this doesn't concern me, I'll get going," I said. "Be careful not to say things you'll regret later."

Hélène gave me a meaningful look. "Don't worry, Silvio."

François didn't reply when I said goodbye. He hadn't budged; he seemed suddenly very old and a certain fragility in his features stood out more than usual; he looked like a man who had been mortally wounded.

I left, but I didn't go home. My heart was beating faster than ever before. My entire past had come back to life. I felt as if I'd been asleep for twenty years and had woken to pick up my book at the very page I'd left off. Without thinking, I went and sat down on the bench beneath the study window, so I could hear every word they said.

For a very long time there was silence. Then he called out, "Hélène . . ."

I was halfhidden by the large rose bush. But I could see right inside the room. I saw the husband and wife sitting next to one another, holding hands; they hadn't said a single word. A single kiss, a single look between them was enough to wipe away any sin. Nevertheless, he questioned her, very quietly, ashamed: "Who was he?"

"He's dead."

"Did I know him?"

"No."

"But you loved him?"

"No. You're the only man I've ever loved. It was before we were married."

"But we were already in love then. At least, I was already in love with you."

"How can I make you understand what it was like?" she cried. "It was over twenty years ago. For a short time I wasn't 'myself'. It was as if . . . as if someone had burst into my life and taken it over. That poor unhappy child accuses me of having forgotten. And it's true, I did forget. Not the facts, of course. Not those terrible months before she was born, not her birth, not the affair . . . But I did forget why I acted the way I did. I can't understand what made me do it any more. It's like a foreign language that you learn and then forget." She spoke passionately, very quickly and quietly.

I was straining to hear, but couldn't make everything out. Then I heard: ". . . To love each other the way we do . . . and then discover the woman you love is someone else."

"But I'm not someone else, François. François, my darling . . . It was the other man who had someone else: a mask, a lie. You and you alone own the true woman. Look at me. I'm the same Hélène who makes you so happy, who has slept in your arms for the past twenty years, who looks after your home, who feels when you're in pain even when you're far away and suffers more than you do, the same woman who spent four years while you were away at war terrified for you, thinking only of you, waiting for you to come back."

She stopped and there was a long silence. Holding my breath, I slipped out of my hiding place and crossed the garden to the road. I was walking quickly. It felt as if some forgotten fire had been rekindled in my body. It was strange: I'd stopped looking at Hélène as a woman such a long time ago. Sometimes I think about the little black woman who was my mistress in the Congo, and the English redhead whose skin was white as milk, who lived with me for two years in Canada . . . But Hélène! Even yesterday it would have been quite an effort of will to think, "But, of course, yes, there was Hélène." She was like those ancient parchments on which the Greeks and Romans wrote erotic stories and which, much later, the monks scraped away at in order to place over the top some illuminated life of a saint. The woman of twenty years ago had disappeared for ever beneath the Hélène of today. The real woman, she'd said. I surprised myself by saying out loud, "No! She's lying."

Afterwards I laughed at myself for being so upset. After all, who knows the real woman? That's the question. The lover or the husband? Are they really so different? Or are they subtly interwoven and inseparable? Are they moulded from two substances that interact to form a third person who doesn't resemble either of them? It all comes down to the same thing: neither the husband nor the lover knows the real woman. Yet the real one is always the most uncomplicated one. But I've lived long enough to know that there's no such thing as uncomplicated emotions.

Not far from my house I ran into a neighbour, old Jault, who was bringing his cows home. We walked together for a while. I could tell he wanted to ask me something but was hesitating. Just as I was about to leave and go inside, he decided to speak. He was absent-mindedly stroking one of his cows, a lovely reddish animal whose horns were in the shape of a lyre. "Is it true what people are saying, that Madame Declos is going to sell her land?"

"I haven't heard anyone say that."

He seemed disappointed. "But they can't go on living around here."

"Why not?" I asked.

"It'd just be better," he muttered vaguely. Then he added, "I heard Monsieur Erard's going to the police — is he? Seems there was something shady about Monsieur Dorin's death and that Marc Ohnet's mixed up in it."

"Certainly not," I replied. "Monsieur Erard is much too sensible to go to the police with no proof but the gossip of a young farmhand. I'm only talking to you now because you seem to know a lot about it, Monsieur Jault. Don't forget that if a man's unjustly accused of something without proof, he can also go to the police and complain about whoever's talking. Understand?"

He picked up his sack and rounded up his animals. "You can't stop people talking," he said bluntly. "Of course, no one around here wants to get mixed up with the police. If the family doesn't do anything, then no one else will do it for them, that's for sure. But since you know Madame Declos and that Marc Ohnet . . ."

"I only know them a little . . ."

"Well, tell them to sell up and go. It'd just be better."

He touched his cap, gave a mumbled goodbye and left.

It was getting dark.

I got home so late, having spent the evening in the village bar, that my housekeeper was worried. I'd been drinking. I'm never normally drunk. Wine is my friend and companion in the wild, isolated place where I live; it satisfies me as a woman might. I belong to a long line of farmers from Burgundy who can knock back a bottle of wine with each meal as if it were baby's milk; alcohol never goes to my head. On this occasion, however, I wasn't my usual self. Instead of soothing me, the wine made me agitated, caused me to feel a kind of rage. It seemed as if my old housekeeper was being deliberately slow. I was desperate for her to leave, as if I were expecting someone. And, in fact, I was: I was expecting my youth. Memories of the past would return to us more often if only we sought them out, sought their intense sweetness. But we let them slumber within us and, worse, we let them die, rot, so much so that the generous impulses that sweep through our souls when we are twenty we later call naive, foolish . . . Our purest, most passionate loves take on the depraved appearance of sordid pleasure.

This evening it wasn't only my memory that relived the past, it was my heart itself. This anger, impatience, this eager thirst for happiness, I remembered them all. Yet no real woman awaited me, just a phantom, created from the same fabric as my dreams. A memory. Intangible, cold. So you need warmth, do you, old man with a withered heart, you need a little fire? I look around at my house and am stunned. I, who used to be so full of energy, so ambitious, can I really be living like this, dragging myself from my bed to my table, then back to my bed again, day after day? How can I live this way? It's as if I no longer exist. I don't think about anything, don't love anything, don't desire anything. There are no newspapers, no books in my house. I fall asleep beside the fire, I smoke my pipe. I stroke my dog. I talk to the housekeeper. That's all, nothing more. I want my youth back. Come back to me, youth. Speak through me. Tell this Hélène who is so sensible, so virtuous, tell her that she was lying. Tell her that the man who loved her isn't dead, that even though she quickly buried me, I'm still alive and I remember everything. She was lying. The real woman hidden inside her, the passionate, happy, daring woman who delighted in pleasure — I'm the only one who really knew her, no one else. François owns only a pale, cold imitation of that woman, as artificial as an epitaph on a tombstone, but I once possessed what is now dead and gone, I possessed her youth.

Come on now . . . that last glass of wine has left me strangely elated. I must get hold of myself. The housekeeper is looking at me in astonishment. The soup has been on the table for a long time, yet I've been sitting here in the kitchen, in the large wicker armchair, scrawling these words, smoking, kicking away the dog who's come over to be stroked. I need to be alone. I don't know why. I can't bear the presence of another human being tonight. All I want are ghosts . . . I'm not hungry. I tell Louise to clear up and go home. She shuts up the hens. All these familiar sounds . . . The shutter that creaks, the latch that squeaks, the sigh of the bucket as it is let down into the well with its bottle of white wine and slab of butter; it will keep them cool until tomorrow. I push away the bottle standing next to me. I push it away, then change my mind; I pick it up again, fill my glass. The wine gives my thoughts clarity. And now, Hélène, now we're alone.

It's exactly what a virtuous woman would say to her husband: "What happened twenty years ago was nothing but a moment of madness." Really? A moment of madness! *I* say that it was the only time you were truly alive. Ever since then you've been pretending, you've gone through the motions of living, but that true passion for life, the kind you savour only once in a lifetime — remember the taste that young lips have: like ripe fruit — you experienced that with me and with me only. "Poor old Silvio, my dear friend, poor Silvio in his rat hole." Is it really true that you forgot me? I have to be fair. I forgot you as well. It took hearing what that young woman said yesterday, and Colette's despair and futile shame and, above all, drinking too much wine to bring you back to me. But the next time I see you I won't let you go so quickly, you can be sure of that. You will hear the truth, you will hear it from me, just as you did in the past when I was the first man to make you understand how beautiful your body was and what a marvellous source of pleasure to you. (You didn't want to, you were shy and innocent back then . . . Still, you gave in. And what a lover you became.) And how we loved each other . . . For, you understand, it's very convenient to say, "I lost my head for a while, it was a few weeks of madness, I shudder to think of it." But you can't erase the truth, and the truth is we loved each other. You loved me so much that you forgot François even existed, so much that you did whatever I wanted in order not to lose me.

Oh, yes, just now you wore the face of an honest, ageing woman, the face of a good mother, shocked to find out that her daughter Colette let another man into her house when her husband was away, into that idyllic Moulin-Neuf. But what did *you* do? She takes after you, your daughter. And the other one too, *she* takes after the two of us. They are both utterly alive, while we have been dead for twenty years; yes, dead, because we don't love anything any more and that's the truth. Because you're not going to try to tell me, are you, that you love François? Of course, he's your friend, your husband, you're used to being together. You could live together as brother and sister. In fact, you surely have lived together as brother and sister since Loulou was born, but you never loved him, you loved me, *me*.

Come here, listen, sit down next to me, think back. Have you really become a hypocrite? Of course not, it's as I thought, you've simply become someone else. How did you put it . . . You were right: at twenty someone bursts into our life. Yes, some winged stranger, leaping, radiant, who sets ablaze our blood, ravages our lives, then disappears. Well, I want to bring that stranger back to life. Listen to him. Look at him. Do you recognise him? Do you remember that long, cold, white corridor and your elderly husband (not François, but your first husband, the one who died so long ago, the one who nobody ever talks about), your husband in his bed with the door left ajar, for he was jealous and suspicious, and how we kissed, you and I, and how the lamp cast that great shadow across the ceiling, the shadow that was you and me, or so we thought? In reality it was neither of us, it was the face of the stranger, like us but different from us, the stranger who disappeared so very long ago.

Hélène, my darling, do you remember the day we met? You were merely a girl when François first saw you. He talked about your past that evening you all came to drink punch with me, when Colette got engaged. I'm not interested in that. You were no child when *I* met you. No, you were a woman, a woman tied to an old man, waiting for him to die so you could marry François. He was gone, living abroad. He had a job teaching French at a university in Bohemia. As for me, I'd just returned from a long journey. You . . . you were young and beautiful, and you were bored. But wait. Let's start from the beginning . . .

Hélène's first husband was a Montrifaut, one of my mother's cousins. I was living in Africa when they married. It was before the 1914 war. Hélène had been a child when I left. Yet I remember that when my mother told me about her marriage — my dear mother wrote to me every week, a kind of diary in which she told me about everyone and everything in the region, in order, no doubt, to make me feel nostalgic so I'd want to come home — I remember that I thought for a long time about that young girl I barely knew. I remember the stifling hot night, the hut, the hurricane lamp in a corner, the lizards chasing flies up the white walls, my black mistress, Fifé, with her green turban. I daydreamed as I read my letter; I pictured the ill-matched couple and found myself saying out loud, "What a shame."

It might be impossible to predict the future, but I believe that certain powerful emotions make themselves felt months, even years, in advance, through a strange quiver in the heart. For example, I only understood the gloomy sadness I had always felt in train stations at dusk when, years later during my time as a soldier in the war, I suddenly recognised it as I waited on a platform for the train that would take me back to the front. In the same way, years before love came into my life, it swept over my heart like a gentle breeze. That night in Africa I was hot, thirsty, feverish. At first I dozed, then I fell into a deep sleep where I dreamt I was with a woman, a Frenchwoman, a young girl from back home. But every time I got close to her she slipped away. I stretched out my arms and, for a second, I could feel her young cheeks, covered in tears. I remember thinking, "Why is this young woman crying? Why won't she let me hold her?" I wanted to pull her close to me but she disappeared. I looked for her through the crowd, the kind of crowd you find at a rural church on Sundays, a crowd of farmers dressed in big black smocks. I still remember one detail: an angry wind was blowing, from God knows where, swelling the farmers' smocks as if they were the sails of a boat. When I woke up I said to myself, "How odd — I just dreamt about that little Hélène who has married Montrifaut," even though, in my dream, I couldn't see the young woman's face.

Two years later I finally returned to France.

I would have continued lodging with my mother if she'd let me live the way I wanted to: spending my days in the woods and my evenings with her. But naturally she wanted to see me married. In these parts marriages are arranged during long, dreary dinners to which all the young women of marriageable age are invited. The men arrive, weighing up in their minds how much the dowry is worth and what the expectations are, in the same way you go to an auction knowing what each item is valued at, but not knowing how high the bidding will go.

Country dinners! Soup thick enough for a spoon to stand up in, enormous pike from the lake on someone's estate, tasty, but so full of bones you feel as if you're eating a thorn bush. And no one says a word. All those thick necks leaning forward and slowly chewing, like cattle in a shed. And after the fish there's the first meat course, preferably roast goose, then the second meat dish, this one cooked in a sauce that gives off an aroma of wine and herbs. Then comes the cheese, which everyone eats from the end of their knives; and to finish off, a pie — apple or cherry, depending on the time of year. Afterwards there's nothing to do but go into the sitting room and choose from among the throng of young women in their pink dresses (before the war all eligible young ladies wore pink dresses, from the candy pink of sugar-coated almonds to the shocking pink of sliced ham), choose from among this crowd of young women, with their little gold necklaces, their hair tied into a chignon at the backs of their necks, with their raw-silk gloves and rough hands, the person with whom you will spend the rest of your life. At that time Cécile Coudray was one such woman. She was thirty-two or thirty-three but still paraded about in the virginal pink dress by her family in the hope of finding her a husband. Poor, dried-up Cécile, with her thin lips, sitting not far from her younger half-sister, who was married and happy.

The first evening I saw Hélène she was wearing a red velvet dress, which was considered rather daring at the time and in that place. She was a young woman with black hair . . . See, I want to describe her, but I can't. No doubt I looked at her too closely right from the start, the way you look at everything you covet. Do you not know the shape and colour of the fruit you bring to your lips? It seems that from the first moment you see the woman you love, she is as close as a kiss. And I loved her. Dark eyes, fair skin, a dress of red velvet, a look of passion, joy and apprehension all at once, that expression of defiance, anxiety and vibrancy, unique to the young . . . I remember . . .

Her husband must have been about the same age as old Declos just before he died, but he wasn't a farmer. My cousin had been a lawyer in Dijon; he was rich; he'd left his post a few months before his marriage and bought the house that Hélène inherited and where she now lives with her second husband and her children. He was a tall, pale old man, frail, with translucent skin; my mother told me he'd been remarkably handsome in the past and well known for his success with women. He barely allowed his young wife to leave his side; if she walked away he would say "Hélène", his voice almost a whisper, and then she . . . Oh, that gesture of annoyance, the way her slender shoulders would suddenly tremble, as a colt trembles when he feels the whip against his coat . . . I think he called her in that way solely for the pleasure of seeing that sign of anger and the satisfaction of feeling she was obeying him. I saw her and I remembered my dream.

I was young then. I wonder if the face of the young man I used to be still lives on in someone's memory?

**110**

Hélène, surely, has forgotten it. But perhaps one of those young women in pink who has grown old and has never seen me again, perhaps she might remember that thin young man, sunburned, with his little black moustache and sharp teeth. I told Colette about that moustache once, to make her laugh. No, I wasn't the typical young man of 1910: straight centre parting, hair slicked down like a wax head at the barber's. I was livelier, stronger, cheerful, more adventurous than even the young people of today. Marc Ohnet bears some resemblance to the man I was. Like him, I was never held back by being overly virtuous. I would have been capable of throwing a jealous husband into the river, capable of drinking, seducing my neighbour's wife, fighting, enduring utter fatigue, the harshest climates. I was young.

So that was our first meeting: a country sitting room with a grand piano, its lid open, so you could see the keys; a young woman dressed in salmon pink — Cécile Coudray — singing "More today than yesterday, but much less than tomorrow"; all the local friends and relations dozing off as they digested, with difficulty, their roast goose and jugged hare; and a woman in a red dress sitting next to me, so close that all I had to do was reach out my hand to touch her, just as in my dream, so close that I could smell her delicate fresh skin, so close and yet so far . . .

As I made my way back home that night long ago, I was determined to see Hélène again, with a plan to seduce her firmly in mind: she was twenty, beautiful and had an old husband; it seemed impossible that she could resist me for long. I imagined innocent meetings at first, then more secret, illicit encounters, then an affair lasting a few months until the moment of my departure. Now that so many years have passed, it is strange to think that our relationship was indeed like that: the way I crudely created it from my dreams and desires. What I could not foresee was the flame that would be locked inside me, whose cinders would continue to glow for years to come, to burn in my heart. How strange it is when something that we have desired so much actually happens. When I was a boy, playing at the beach, I remember a game I loved, which was an omen of my future life. I would dig a channel with high sides in the sand for the sea to fill. But when it came, the water flooded the path I had created for it with such violence that it destroyed everything in its way: my castles made of pebbles, my dykes of sand. It swept away everything, destroying it all, then disappeared, leaving me with a heavy heart, yet not daring to ask for pity, since the sea had only responded to my call. It's the same with love. You call out for it, you plan its course. The wave crashes into your heart, but it's so different from how you imagined it, so bitter and icy.

I tried to see Hélène at her husband's house. Needing an excuse, I remembered that she grew magnificent roses in her garden. They were crimson, full-bodied roses with long stems and sharp thorns as hard as steel. They gave off very little fragrance but had this familiar, sturdy look about them, something plump and bright, like the cheek of a beautiful country girl. I made up some story. I wanted to surprise my mother by ordering the same rose bushes for her in town. I used this as a pretext to go to Hélène's house in order to ask her the exact name of the flowers.

She greeted me wearing no hat beneath the blazing sun, a pair of secateurs in her hand. Since then, I have seen her stand exactly like that so many times. Even now she has the windswept beauty of a peach tree, delicate skin that has hardly ever been powdered but turns golden in the fresh air and sunshine.

She told me that her husband wasn't well. He had begun the long illness that would afflict him for two more years before leaving her a widow. His vanity made him close his bedroom door to keep his wife out when he was suffering from an attack: he had the kind of asthma old people get, painful and choking. Later on, when he could no longer get out of bed, he insisted she always sit with him. But at the time I'm talking about she was still free to tell me the name of those roses and show me into a large sitting room whose shutters were half-closed, where a bumble-bee buzzed about a bouquet of flowers. I remember that the house, even then, had its sweet smell of fresh wax, lavender and jam simmering in enormous pans.

I asked permission to see her again. I saw her once, twice, ten times more. I waited for her at the edge of the village, or at the church door on Sundays; on the river bank, in the woods and at the Moulin-Neuf where Colette . . . She's forgotten that. The mill hadn't yet been renovated back then. It was old and gloomy, despite being called the "New Mill". Its crumbling walls, not far from Coudray and surrounded by the roar of the river, often witnessed our visits to the miller's wife. A few days after I first met Hélène, her stepmother had died when the horse pulling the trap she was driving veered into a ditch; being exceedingly mean, she had wished to make use of an animal she'd bought cheap, but which was too young to be harnessed. Cécile's face was horribly injured; the mother fractured her skull and died on the road. Cécile inherited the little estate at Coudray and a small income. She had always been unsociable and shy; the injuries that disfigured her removed any self-confidence she might have had. She refused to see anyone, believing that people were making fun of her. In the space of a few months she became the odd creature I knew towards the end of her life: thin and anxious looking, with a limp and a head that jerked endlessly from side to side, like an old bird. Hélène often visited her at Coudray and, since I knew this, I found excuses to go to Cécile's house every day and see the good woman; then I would walk Hélène back to the edge of the woods.

One day, as I was watching the clock and trying to prolong my visit, Cécile said, "Hélène won't be coming today."

I protested that I hadn't come for Hélène . . . She stood up and crossed the room. Her finger automatically traced the curved back of an armchair to check for dust (her mother had trained her in every aspect of housekeeping and she was always worried about it: she wandered nervously about the room, adjusting a curtain here, blowing on a tarnished mirror there, straightening a flower, anxiously jerking her head from side to side as if she expected to see her mother lurking in the shadows, spying on her). "Monsieur Sylvestre," she said, emotion in her voice, "no one has ever come to this house to see only me . . . Until I was seventeen I never gave it a thought. Then young men began to visit. Some of them came because of the maid, others because of the gardener's daughter, who was blonde and pretty; then, when Hélène grew up, they came for her. It's still the same. It doesn't surprise me. But I don't want people mocking me. Just tell me that you want to see Hélène and I'll tell you myself the days and times I'm expecting her." She spoke with a kind of restrained anger that was painful to hear.

"Do you love your sister?" I asked.

"She isn't my sister. She's a stranger to me. But I've known her since she was a baby and I love her, yes, I do love her. She's no happier than I am, actually," she said, somewhat gratified. "Everyone has their problems."

"Please don't think that she knows my intentions . . . I'd be devastated if you thought there was some kind of complicity . . ."

She shook her head. "Hélène is a faithful woman," she said.

"Really? Her husband is so old: he couldn't possibly hope for her to be faithful. It would be monstrous of him, given the circumstances," I said passionately. "She's twenty and he's more than sixty. Such a marriage can only be explained by desperation."

"That's exactly what it was. You see, Hélène was my father's daughter from his first marriage and my mother . . ."

"I understand, but do you really think that, under these circumstances, it's reasonable to expect fidelity?"

Her eyes flashed at me. "I didn't say it was to her husband that she would remain faithful."

"What! To whom, then?"

"That you can ask her yourself."

Once again she limped across the Coudray sitting room, bumping into furniture like a night owl trapped in a bedroom. Now that I think about it and recall the expression she had on her face then, Brigitte's story is suddenly clear to me, lit up in a sinister, fiendish light, laying bare the very soul of that ageing woman. She was never able to forgive Hélène for having been loved more than her. She reminds me of one of my relatives, who once said something horrible. She had taken a poor countrywoman under her wing, giving her food,

**116**

shoes, sweets, toys for her children. Then, one day, the woman told her she was going to get married again — she had lost her husband during the war — to a kind, handsome young man who was as poor as she was. Immediately the benefactress stopped her visits. Some time later they ran into each other and the woman gently scolded her ("Madame seems to have forgotten about me"), at which my relative curtly replied, "My dear Jeanne, I hadn't realised you were happy."

Cécile Coudray, who saved Hélène's honour and maybe even her life when she thought she was in dire straits, was never able to forgive her for being happy. It's only human.

"Tell me what you mean," I begged her in anguish.

But the old bird just flapped her dark wings at me. She was still dressed in mourning for her mother; her black crêpe veil fluttered around her. I left Coudray, more passionately in love than I had ever been. And the restraint towards Hélène which had held me back disappeared; I began to woo her in earnest . . . Oh, back then it was done so sweetly, so properly. Nothing like the brutal way young people say they love each other these days. I imagine Marc Ohnet would have found it amusing. But in the end it all comes down to the same thing, the same desire . . . the same roaring, all-consuming tidal wave of love.

Hélène listened to me with deep, sorrowful solemnity. "Cécile was telling you the truth. I do love someone."

Then she told me about how she'd met François, how he'd fallen in love with her when she was still nearly a child, how he'd gone away, about her own unhappiness in her family and, finally, how she'd married an older man and how François had come back. They hadn't wanted to betray her elderly husband. They had parted.

"So now you're waiting for your husband to die?" I asked.

She went slightly pale, then nodded. "He's forty years older than me," she said quietly. "It would be ridiculous to pretend I love him. But I'm not hoping he'll die. I'm doing my best to look after him. To him, I'm . . ." She hesitated. "I'm a friend, a young woman, a nurse, all of that. But not a wife. Not his wife. But I want to be faithful to him in spite of all that, and not just physically, but in my soul. That's why François and I decided to part. He accepted a job abroad. We don't even write to each other. I'm doing my duty here. If my husband dies, François will wait a few months before coming back. We won't rush anything. We don't want to cause a scandal. He'll come back and we'll get married. If my husband lives for many years to come, well, that's my hard luck. My youth will be gone and all my hopes for happiness, but at least I won't have a vile act on my conscience. As for you . . ."

"As for me," I said, "the best thing for me to do is leave at once."

She said what all women say at such times: that I shouldn't hold it against her, that she hadn't been flirting; it was just that she felt so lonely, all friendship was precious to her and we could be friends . . . But I could think of only one thing: she loved another man and I was in pain. My love affair was over.

That was in 1912. I went back to Africa for two years, then returned to France a few months before the war. My mother had died, but my cousin Montrifaut was still alive. I went to visit him. He was very ill and near the end, or so we all hoped. It was only the injections that were keeping him going. He was unbearably demanding, with bouts of anger that bordered on madness.

"He's unhappy and he takes it out on everyone else," people said.

They all praised Hélène for the way she behaved.

"She won't have to go on suffering much longer," whispered all the ladies in the region, and they sighed with both pity and envy, imagining how much Hélène would inherit.

But I found out something that no one else knew: old Montrifaut was leaving only a small part of his fortune to his young wife; the rest was going to his brother's family. Hélène knew all about these arrangements, but she was (and still is) the sort of woman whose altruism is indisputable, a part of who she is. Hélène wouldn't be Hélène if she could act out of personal interest and François is the same. So

Hélène knew that her devotion would reap no reward and it was that very fact that forced her to push this devotion to the extreme. She had a great need to respect herself.

"Actually," she told me, "he's been good for me, in spite of everything."

The sick man suffered exhausting fits of asthma, but when I saw him he complained most about his terrible insomnia. He was sitting up in bed (his bedroom has since become the sitting room), wearing a scarf around his head, the way invalids used to. He was terrifying and strange, the shadow of his large, pinched nose looming above him on the wall. A small lamp was lit beside his bed. His voice was no more than a whisper. "Yes," he said, "just imagine . . . I haven't slept in two months. It's horrible. It makes my life twice as long."

"What are you complaining about?" I cried. "Ten lives wouldn't be enough for me!"

And it was true. I felt so strong, back then, as if my body was built to last a hundred years.

I looked at Hélène as I said it.

Hélène sighed and that involuntary sigh said so many things. She was pale and thin, and less beautiful than two years before. You could see that she needed exercise and fresh air, that she'd been confined to the sickroom. When she first saw me she remained calm and smiled as she always did, but when she shook my hand, when she spoke the banal words of welcome, her voice betrayed her: it broke suddenly, leaving a gap in the vague, kind words she spoke; it was as if the timbre of her voice had changed, as if her blood had unexpectedly rushed to her heart. And when I answered her I could hear my own voice breaking the same way. We stood beside the sick man's bed and looked at each other, I with barely disguised triumph, she with a sort of despair. And that sigh! It meant she understood me, that she envied my freedom, that she too, in another time and place, would have liked ten lives and to live each one to the full, but instead she watched days and years pass, all lost to love.

When she walked me to the door I asked if she'd heard from François.

She glanced anxiously towards the dying man's bed. "He never writes to me," she said.

"He keeps to the same arrangement?"

"Yes. François won't change."

I wonder now how right she was. How was François spending those hot spring days in that little village in Bohemia? Surely there was some pretty country girl, some young servant in the background? After all, the three of us were young. It wasn't just about the pleasures of the flesh. No, it wasn't that simple. The flesh is easy to satisfy. It's the heart that is insatiable, the heart that needs to love, to despair, to burn with any kind of fire . . . That was what we wanted. To burn, to be consumed, to devour our days just as fire devours the forest.

It was the most beautiful spring evening of 1914. The door stood open behind us and we could see the shadow of a large, pinched nose on the wall. We were standing in the white corridor where, in years since, Hélène has stood before me so many times, her children hanging on to her skirt, saying in her polite, calm voice, "Oh, it's you, my dear Silvio, come in. There's an extra egg and a veal cutlet. Would you like to stay for lunch?"

"My dear Silvio . . ." That's not what she called me then. She simply said "Silvio" (the word itself was a caress), "will you be staying home for long?"

I didn't answer but pointed instead to the shadow of the dying man and asked, "Is it very hard?"

She shuddered. "Quite hard, yes, but I don't want people feeling sorry for me."

"But he'll die soon," I stressed cruelly. "François will come back."

"Yes," she said, "he'll come back. But it would have been better if he'd never gone away."

"Are you still in love with him?"

We were talking without knowing what we were saying. Our lips were moving, but they were lying. Only our eyes spoke, understood each other. But when I took her in my arms, our lips finally told the truth.

I will never forget that moment, never. It was then that I saw our shadows, merging as one, on the whitewashed wall. There were lamps all along the corridor, keeping watch. All along that big, bare corridor shadows danced, swayed and disappeared.

"Hélène," the dying man called out, "Hélène."

We didn't move. She seemed to be drinking me in, breathing in my heart. As for me, by the time I finally let her go I knew I had already begun to love her less.

# A Partisan's Daughter

## Louis de Bernières

Set in North London during the Winter of Discontent, A Partisan's Daughter features the relationship between Chris, an unhappily-married, middle-aged Englishman and Roza, a young Serbian woman who has recently moved to London.

While driving through Archway in the course of his job as a medical rep, Chris is captivated by a young woman on a street corner. Clumsily, he engages her in conversation, and he secures an invitation to return one day for a coffee. His visits become more frequent and Roza starts to tell him the story of her life, drawing him increasingly into her world — from her childhood as a daughter of one of Tito's partisans, through her journey to England and on to her more recent colourful and dangerous past in London.

ISBN 978-0-7531-8156-0 (hb)
ISBN 978-0-7531-8157-7 (pb)

# Consequences

## Penelope Lively

*A hugely satisfying and romantic novel.*

Three generations of 20th-century women: a young woman, her daughter and her granddaughter, their contrasting lives and their achievement of love.

Lorna escapes her conventional Kensington family to marry artist Matt, but the Second World War puts an end to their immense happiness. Molly, their daughter, will have to wait longer to find love and Ruth, Lorna's granddaughter, even longer still: an enthralling examination of interweaving love and history.

**ISBN 978-0-7531-7992-5 (hb)**
**ISBN 978-0-7531-7993-2 (pb)**